'Have you ever seen a ghost?'

'No, but…'

Scary tales from a Liverpool Cabbie.

Dedicated to my beautiful Mum,
Jean O'Hare

Jumped or Pushed?

I once met a lad called Ian, when I was on holiday in Turkey. I can't call him a great friend because I only knew him for two weeks. However, for those two weeks, my family and his family became good friends and he didn't strike me as the type to make up fanciful stories. One night, over a few drinks, I was telling Ian that I had just passed my degree in Psychology at University and that my favourite subject had been "The Psychology of the Paranormal."

"Ghosts?" he said.

"Yeah, stuff like that," I replied.

"I have never told anyone this before," he continued. "When my Mum was on her death bed, she told me I had, 'the gift'. I just thought it must be the ramblings of a dying woman, because she had never mentioned it before and I had never experienced anything unusual, or seen any ghosts."

Ian then told me that his wife Dawn, who was with us on the holiday, was in fact his second wife. His first wife was called Ann and he and Ann spent their honeymoon in

Spain. When they arrived at their hotel they could see that it was at least twenty stories high. They checked in at reception and were allocated a room near the top.

As soon as they entered the room, his new wife headed straight for the bathroom. It was very late in the day and she was keen to go out and enjoy what was left of the evening. Ian, however, just sat on the edge of the bed looking around the room. For the first time in his life, Ian felt very scared by something he couldn't even see. Although he couldn't see anyone, he had a really nauseating feeling that someone was stood just feet away, staring at him.

Ian was truly terrified. The hairs on his arms and the back of his neck were stood on end. He had never experienced anything like this before and he didn't like it one little bit. His wife came out of the bathroom and was pretty annoyed that he hadn't changed his clothes yet.

"Come on," she scowled, "get ready or it won't be worth going out."

"I'll go like this," Ian whispered.

"What?"

"I said I'm not getting changed. Come on if you're ready, let's just go. I don't like it in here."

"What on earth is the matter with you?"

"Nothing, let's just go." And with that he ushered her out of the door.

Ian breathed a huge sigh of relief as he and his wife walked along the hotel corridor towards the elevator. Then his worst fears were confirmed, when the invisible entity shoved him in the back!

"Get off me!" Ian screamed at thin air.

"What the hell are you doing?" his wife asked in amazement.

Ian grabbed her by the arm and hurried her along the corridor. Then the invisible thing pushed him so hard he fell to his knees!

"Leave me alone!" Ian shouted, as he scrambled to his feet and dragged his wife into the elevator.

"Ian what's wrong with you? I've never seen you like this before."

"Someone shoved me in the back."

"Don't be ridiculous, there was nobody in the corridor but us."

Suddenly the elevator doors opened.

"Come on," said Ian, "I need a drink."

As they sat in a local bar having a few drinks, Ian told Ann the whole story.

"You're probably just a bit stressed or something," his wife tried to reason. "Whatever," said Ian, "but I'll tell you

3

something. I am not going back in that room. I am going to ask the hotel to switch us to another room."

After a few more drinks, checking out the different bars, Ian began to relax a little and had quite a good time. That was until it was time to go back to the hotel. As soon as they entered the hotel lobby, Ian headed straight for the reception desk and rang the bell.

"What are you doing?" his wife asked.

"I'm going to ask them to move us."

"Oh Ian please, I'm tired and there is no one here anyway. Let's ask in the morning, eh love?"

Reluctantly, Ian followed her into the elevator. As they walked along the corridor to their room, his wife watched in amazement as Ian fell violently to the floor once again!

"Stop it!" Ian screamed, "Why are you doing this to me?"

Ann started to cry and Ian suddenly realised what this must seem like to her.

"I'm sorry, Babe," he said, as he clambered to his feet and put his arms around her.

"Why are you acting like this?" she sobbed.

"I'm sorry, I really am. But someone pushed me over again."

Ian cuddled her in bed until she fell asleep, but Ian couldn't even close his eyes never mind sleep. Whatever it was, was standing in the room staring at him! He couldn't see it, but he could feel its eyes burning into him. What happened next is enough to frighten the life out of even the most ardent non believer.

Ian says, "I must have fallen asleep, when suddenly my eyes shot wide open and I found myself leaning over the balcony, staring at the street twenty floors below!"

He instinctively threw himself backwards and landed on his backside on the hotel room floor. Enough was enough and Ian sat in a chair chain smoking until daylight, with Mr. Invisible continuing to stare at him intently.

Ian was already waiting at the reception desk when the staff came on duty.

"I want to change rooms."

"I'm sorry, Sir. We are fully booked."

"You don't understand. I cannot stay in that room."

"I am sorry sir; I can't give you a room I don't have."

Ian waited in the reception until the holiday rep arrived.

"I want to move rooms," he begged her.

"The hotel is fully booked."

"Then I need to move hotel."

"Why?" asked the Rep, "are you ok?"

Ian sat her down and told her everything that had happened the night before.

"Bloody hell," was all she could manage to say, as she stared at him open mouthed. Later that day, the rep found Ian and Ann a new room at a different hotel.

The second hotel was much classier than the first and he and Ann had a fantastic honeymoon. As Ian climbed aboard the coach to the airport going home, he smiled at the holiday Rep. "I can't thank you enough," he told her.

"That's Okay," she smiled back. But as Ian went to take his seat on the coach, the rep grabbed his arm.

"Listen," she whispered, "I want to have a quiet word with you at the airport, in private Ok?"

"Ok," he nodded. He could see how serious she was and he took his seat wondering what the hell was going to happen now?

At the airport, Ian told Ann to go and join the queue at check in, saying he just wanted to thank the rep for helping them. She swallowed the story and went to join the queue, while Ian hung around the coach until the last of the holiday makers had trundled away.

"Listen" the rep whispered, "Please don't tell anyone what I am about to tell you, because if you do I will get the sack."

"Don't worry," Ian promised, "I just want to get home."

"The reason you got upgraded to a better hotel, was because my boss was terrified you were going to sue him after I told him what had happened to you. The room you stayed in had been empty for two weeks while the police forensic team checked it out. The last person to stay in that room was a young lad, who killed himself by jumping off the balcony."

Ian stared into the young rep's eyes trying to take it all in. He could see how scared she was. Terrified of how he was going to react and whether she was going to lose her job or not.

"Listen," Ian said, taking hold of her hand. "Don't worry, I am not going to try to sue your boss or anything, your secret is safe with me. You might want to do something for me though?"

"Sure," she said, "What?"

"Try having a word with your boss, or the police, or whoever. Try and get someone to have a deeper look into what happened in that room. Because I think that young lad was trying to tell me that he never jumped off that balcony. He was pushed!

Biker Boy

One day, whilst working in my taxi, I was parked up on a pub car park waiting for my next 'job'. I was reading a book of ghost stories when another taxi driver pulled up alongside me. It was John and John and his brothers had been really good to me since I was knee high to a grasshopper, so I put the book down to talk to him.

"What are you reading?" he asked.

"A book about ghosts," I said.

"Ghosts?"

"Yeah. Have you ever seen a ghost?"

"No. I don't believe in them," he said.

Then he turned to me and said, "A strange thing happened a few years ago, though."

I thought, "Here we go." Everyone has had something strange happen to them. Haven't they? But then he told me this amazing tale.

One lazy Saturday afternoon John was at home watching the horse racing on the television, as he had had a little flutter, when much to his annoyance there was a knock at the front door. John opened the door to find a very dark skinned woman, possibly African, judging by her clothes and headscarf, standing on his doorstep.

"Hello," she said. "Please forgive me for bothering you like this. It's just that I used to live in this house when I was a child and as I was in the area, visiting a sick relative in the hospital up the road, I couldn't resist knocking in the hope that you may allow me to take a peek inside?"

John was a bit perturbed, especially as he was missing his horse racing, but what could he say? "Sure, step inside," and John then proceeded to show the lady the living room, kitchen and garden on the ground floor.

"It is just how I remember it," she said. "Obviously the wallpaper has changed, but it's all still here. Would you mind if I took a look upstairs?"

"Oh, I don't know," said John, who quite truthfully pointed out that his wife was not feeling too well and was having a 'lay down' on the bed upstairs. At this point John's wife entered the room saying she had heard him talking to someone. John introduced the stranger in their home and explained what she was doing there.

"Well, I am up now," said John's wife. "Come with me, I will show you the upstairs."

The lady stranger was filled with nostalgia as she wondered about the upstairs rooms, explaining how, "this was her mother and father's room and this was her brother's room." Then she stopped at the foot of another stairway and, suddenly looking very nervous, asked if she could go up to the attic room!

John and his wife looked at each other. "Okay," said John's wife, "but I must warn you, that is my son's room and it is usually quite a mess." On reaching the top of the stairs, the stranger pushed open the attic bedroom door and stood surveying its interior, with John and his wife stood behind her.

"Yes," she said. "This is where it happened!"

Luckily, both John and his wife were not the type of people to be immediately spooked by something and almost smiled at each other as they both thought, "this is getting interesting."

"Where? What happened, love?" John asked.

"Oh, I am sorry," said the lady. "I have said too much, haven't I? It was not my intention to alarm you. Thank you so much for showing me around. I shall not keep you any longer."

"Hold on a second," said John's wife. "You said something happened in this room, I would appreciate it if you told me what!"

"Please," pleaded the stranger.

"No, please," demanded John's wife.

"Very well," conceded the lady. "Have you ever seen anything strange in this room?"

"Like what?" enquired John's wife.

"Like a ghost?" the stranger asked.

John and his wife again looked at each other, only this time their wry smiles were gone.

"No," said John. "Why?"

The African lady then told them that the attic room had been her younger sister's room. One day her younger sister had trotted up the stairs to her room and upon pushing open the door, began to scream hysterically. Her younger sister was so traumatised by what she had seen that she ended up being admitted to a psychiatric ward at the hospital. After a period of time the staff on the ward were able to ascertain that the young girl claimed to have seen a teenage boy, dressed in black leather and with blood all over his face, in her bedroom!

After the lady had left, again apologising if she had upset them, John and his wife pondered on what had just happened. John's wife quickly dismissed the episode and went back upstairs to rest. John went back to watching the horse racing, but he could not stop thinking about what the African lady had said. When the racing had finished, John stood up and looked out of the living room window. Across the street he could see his neighbour Peter cutting the lawn. He suddenly had an idea!

He opened the front door and crossed the street to talk to Peter.

"Hi Pete, how is your Mum?"

"She is okay, thanks. She is not getting any younger, but she is hanging in there."

"Can I have a quick word with her?" John asked.

"Sure, why?"

"I just want to ask her about some people who lived in my house before me."

Peter called his mum and she came to the front gate to greet John. After asking how she was John asked, "Winnie, you have lived here most of your life, haven't you?"

"Oh, yes," says Winnie, "since I was a little girl. We were one of the first families to move in round here you know? When they were first built."

"Winnie, I need to ask you something," said John, trying to be as diplomatic as he could, considering Winnie's age. "Do you remember a black family that used to live in my house?"

"Ooh yes," she says. "Terrible what happened to them, it was."

"What happened to them, Winnie?"

"Well," she said, "folk round here, most of them had never seen black people before and they did not like it. Hounded them out they did, threw bricks through the front windows. They were not easily scared off, but in the end they took up and left."

"Have you ever heard of a ghost in my house?" John

asked.

"A ghost!" exclaimed Winnie, "No, why?"

John then told Winnie of the African lady that had called to his house that day, and of her claims that her younger sister had seen the ghost of a young man dressed in black leather.

"Oh, now then," said a shocked Winnie, "Now that is interesting!"

"What is, Winnie?" John asked, now totally captivated by the old lady.

What Winnie then told John could possibly be the final piece in the jigsaw to this intriguing tale.

Winnie told John that she remembered the young African girl being carried into an ambulance screaming hysterically, but none of the neighbours bothered to ask why.

Then she told John that before the African family lived in his house, another family had lived there who had a teenage son. The son loved motorbikes and always wore the traditional black leather biker's jacket and black leather trousers.

One day, he stole a motorbike and sidecar from the local coal colliery at Cronton, while the miners were at work. He drove the motorbike at break neck speed down the hill that is called, "Dragon Lane", straight past what is now John's house, but back then was the young biker's house.

He then lost control of the motorbike, possibly because it

had the sidecar attached and he wasn't used to it. In any case, he crashed headlong into the solid sandstone walls of The Carrs Hotel public house, killing him instantly.

My mate John still lives in the house and just laughs off something that happened one day in his life saying, "I've never seen any ghosts."

However, his older brother Barry once had nowhere to live and John let him stay in the attic room until he sorted himself out. Barry eventually found himself a new home and was pleased to be leaving John's attic room.

"There is definitely something not right in that room," Barry told me. "One night I was lying in bed in the dark, when I heard something being dragged across the floor. I switched the light on and a heavy wooden blanket chest had been dragged into the middle of the room."

Woody's house

When I was 13 years old, I was out riding my prized Gold Raleigh Scorpio racing bike that my parents had scrimped and saved to buy for me for Christmas. My mum shouted my name so I rode over to her.

"Here," she said, "take this money down to the church and give it to your sister. She has forgotten to take the money to pay for her day trip."

"Oh, Mum," I moaned.

"Just do it and hurry up," she commanded, and so with a sigh I headed off for the church. I found my little sister and gave her the money.

"What are you doing here?" I asked her.

"Choir practice," she replied.

"Choir practice," I laughed, "I didn't know you were religious?"

"I'm not," she told me, "but there is a youth club straight after choir practice, and if you are already in the building, you don't have to pay to get in."

"You crafty little sod," I laughed, "any good is it? This youth club?"

"Yeah, you would love it. It's got table tennis and pool tables and all sorts of games."

"How much is it to get in?" I asked her.

"Why don't you just stay for choir practice and get in for free?" she suggested.

"Get lost," I said, "I'm not singing any stupid songs."

"You don't have to sing, just sit and pretend. It's only for an hour."

And so, with no money to get into the youth club otherwise, I had no choice and sat down with the choir. As they started singing the first song, I followed the words on my hymn sheet, and then I glanced around at the other people. Two lads, about the same age as me, or maybe a little older, were sitting there staring at me and whispering to each other.

All young boys will know that feeling. When you just know that they are going to give you a good kicking, as soon as there are no adults watching. I wanted to get out of there, but I was too embarrassed to just get up and walk out. So I sat through an excruciating hour, not daring to make eye contact with the two boys.

As soon as the choir practice ended, I decided to abandon the youth club and get out of there. But I needed to get my bike, which I had hidden in a room at the back of the church. I took the lock off my bike and spun it around to face the door, but it was too late. The two boys were stood in the doorway and they had me trapped, with no adults around to save me.

As they moved in for the kill, I dropped my bike and started to fight back. After taking a few punches, the bigger of the two lads got behind me and grabbed me in a vice-like grip.

"Okay, mate," he said, "take it easy. You're quite a little fighter aren't you? You didn't look like you had it in you."

"Get off me," I snarled.

"Or you will do what, exactly?" he laughed. "Okay, mate, I am going to let you go. Don't do anything stupid now, or you and I will really start fighting. Okay?" And so, he released me from his strong grip. "What's your name?" he asked.

"Carle."

"I'm Paul and this is Woody. Are you staying for the youth club?"

"Why?" I asked, "So you can beat me up again later?"

"Nah, sorry about that mate, just wanted to see what you were made of. We wouldn't have really hurt ya. A word of warning though, if you are thinking of staying, there are some pretty tough lads come in here. You can hang around with us if you want to."

And thus began a friendship that continues to this day. Paul and Woody are still my two best friends and the three of us are now 50 years old. Which is why, when we were 19 years old and the pair of them told me the following amazing tale, I believed them.

Woody was 19 and was working down the coal mine as an apprentice fitter, when he met and fell head over heels in love with a girl called Sandra and asked her to marry him. A delighted Sandra said yes and the couple became engaged. A few days later, Woody was in the canteen at work when one of the other miners came over to Woody's table. Woody only knew him to let on to, he had never had a conversation with the man.

"Congratulations," he said to Woody, "I believe you are engaged to be married?"

"Yes, we are," Woody replied, "thank you for your well wishes."

"I suppose you will be looking to buy a house now then?" the miner queried.

"I guess so," Woody replied, "We haven't really discussed that far ahead."

"It's just that I have got a house for sale, you see," said the miner as he pulled up a chair. "I need to sell it quick because I have already moved into another house. It is up for sale for £23,000 but if you were interested, I could knock £5,000 off the asking price and let you have it for £18,000."

"That sounds like a bit of a bargain?" Woody queried, suspiciously.

"It is," the miner replied, "but like I said, I have already bought another house and I had to take out a bridging loan to cover the two mortgages. The repayments are killing me, which is why I would be willing to drop the price for you. You being a work colleague and all that."

"Well, it's got to be worth a look at least," Woody said, "I will talk to you after work."

After the shift, the miner came up to Woody in the changing rooms. "Here," he said, "here is the address and here are the keys. The place is empty, so you and your girlfriend can go around there any time you want to. Just let me have the keys back when you are done."

"Okay," said Woody. "Thanks very much. I will let you know as soon as."

The next day Woody pulled into the driveway of the miner's house on his motorbike, with Sandra riding pillion.

"Hey, are you sure this is it?" Sandra smiled, "It looks lovely, and what a lovely address, number one Paradise Close."

"Yeah, It does look good doesn't it? Woody said as he pulled off his crash helmet. "When he said £18,000 I thought it would be a right dump, but this estate looks like it hasn't been built very long. Looks like a lovely little area doesn't it?"

"Yeah, it looks fab," Sandra agreed, "come on let's see if the inside is as good as the outside."

"Oh, Andy look at this," Sandra gasped as she walked into the living room. "I love it. Oh, look, there is a bar under the stairs. Oh and look at this kitchen. That mate of yours must be mad. Are you sure he only wants £18,000 for this place?"

"That's what he said."

"Then I think we should snap his hand off, it is well worth that. It is even cheap at the £23,000 he has got it advertised for."

"I agree," Woody smiled, "shall I tell him yes then?"

"Yes," Sandra squealed, and she dived into Woody's arms and wrapped her legs around his waist. "We have got our own house!"

With their joint income, Woody and Sandra had no problem securing a mortgage and the deal with the miner was done. Woody's mum and dad bought the happy couple a settee, which was placed in the living room of the empty house. Sandra's mum and dad bought them a double bed, which Woody set up in the main bedroom. However, Sandra announced that she did not want to move in until they were married.

"You are probably right," Woody agreed, "It will give us a chance to save some money, if we both stay at our parents for a while."

Secretly, Woody was thrilled. This meant more nights out with 'The Boys', before he tied the dreaded knot. Over the next few weeks, 'The Boys', myself included, would go drinking in the town close to Woody's house. When the bars closed, we would 'crash' back at Woody's virtually empty house, munching on a takeaway of burger and chips. I personally found the place to be very spooky, but I just put it down to the fact that we only had candles for light, as the electricity was not turned on.

On another occasion, only Paul and Woody were out drinking, close to Woody's uninhabited house. After purchasing the usual burger and chips, the pair of them staggered back to the house. Sitting in the candle light eating their food, Woody went behind the bar under the stairs.

"Hey Paul, there is some whiskey in a bottle here."

"Nice one. Are there any glasses?"

Paul and Woody sat laughing, drinking whiskey and eating chips.

"I'm done in, ya know?" said Paul, lying back on the settee.

"Yeah, I'm gonna crash out as well. Are you okay on the settee?"

"Yeah, see ya in the morning," Paul replied and Woody went upstairs and lay down on the bed.

Woody takes up the story; "I was laying there awake, just thinking about things and waiting for sleep to come, when suddenly I heard someone sneaking up the stairs. I thought Paul was going to try to scare me, but he was only using the toilet. I heard him close the door and put the little bolt on. Just as I was beginning to relax, I heard someone run across the landing outside my bedroom, followed by an almighty crash. For a few seconds the silence was deafening and then Paul's voice came from the bathroom."

"Woody, stop it now, that really scared me."

"What are you talking about?"

"You effing well know what I am talking about and it's not funny, that could have seriously hurt me."

"Paul, I swear I have not left my bed, I don't know what you are talking about."

"Then you better come and have a look at this," Paul replied.

Woody walked out onto the landing and through the dim light of a street lamp shining in from outdoors, he could see the shadow of Paul sitting on the toilet.

"Look at the door," Paul said, and Woody walked towards the bathroom door. It had been completely kicked in, and was hanging by one hinge.

"What were you thinking of?" Paul demanded to know.

"Paul, I swear that wasn't me."

"Well, I don't know about you," Paul said pulling up his trousers. "I'm not staying here. I'm going to see if I can flag down a cab."

"Good idea," Woody agreed, "I'm coming with you."

It took a few days before Woody finally plucked up the courage to go round to the house again. And sure enough there it was, the bathroom door hanging from one hinge.

He quickly assessed what tools he would need to fix it and returned the next day to put it right, without telling Sandra what had happened.

As it turned out, Woody didn't need to tell Sandra anyway. Because not long after, Sandra broke Woody's heart by declaring that she was not ready for marriage, and she wanted to split up. She also wanted him to sell the house and split any profits with her.

Woody's older sister Louise placed a comforting hand on her younger brother's shoulder as he cried over his lost love.

"All will seem better in the morning," she promised him. Then she pounced for what she was really after. "Maybe me and Terry could help you out?"

"How do you mean? Woody asked.

"Well me and Terry are looking for a bigger place to bring the kids up in; we could give you the £18,000 that you paid for it?"

"Oh, thanks Louise, and here's me thinking that you actually care."

"I do care!"

"No you don't and if you want the bloody house you can have it. I will talk to Sandra about your offer."

Sandra said, "No way." She wanted at least £22,000. That equated to £2,000 profit for both Woody and herself.

"Oh, now I get it," it suddenly dawned on Woody. "You have just passed your driving test and you want the £2,000 to buy a car. Well I hope it was worth losing me and the house for," and he slammed down the phone.

Woody held a family meeting with his sister Louise and his brother-in-law Terry, with Woody and Louise's old dad as the referee.

Woody explained that Sandra wanted £2,000. He personally did not want to make any money out of his sister. £20,000 and the house was theirs. And as a house warming gift from Woody, they could keep the well stacked bags of coal that Woody had been bringing home from work and stacking in the garage. The house had coal-fired central heating and Woody estimated that there was nearly a thousand pounds worth of coal.

Louise and Terry hugged and their old dad said, "I'll put the kettle on then shall I? That was easy enough, nice to have a happy ending."

Except it was far from a happy ending.

Louise, Terry and the children moved into the house and despite being extremely happy at first, it did not take long for Louise to become worried. Louise is a very spiritual type of person at the best of times, and she was beginning to get a sense that all was not quite right.

Not long after they moved in, Louise and Terry were lying in bed stroking each other's faces and giggling like teenagers, as they had just quietly made love. The children were fast asleep in their rooms. Suddenly, the chilling sound of a woman screaming for help rang out in the street, right outside Terry and Louise's bedroom window. They both jumped up and looked out of the window, but there was nobody there.

"We are not hearing things, Terry," Louise said, "she must be behind the hedge, come on let's go and see." Terry opened the front door and quickly covered the driveway in his bare feet. He looked up and down the close. "There is no one here."

"Ok," Louise said, "Come back in," and she caught a glimpse of the lady who lived opposite peeping through her curtains. The lady quickly dropped the curtains when she realised that Louise had spotted her.

Over the next few weeks, Louise would be woken at night by noises in the kitchen. There, she would find a cup smashed across the floor, or the lids of her sauce pans scattered across the worktops.

Louise thought to seek the advice of a young priest in the local church, who called round and blessed the house while the children were at school.

Then one night, the noise was so bad that even Terry woke up.

"What's that?"

"I think someone is breaking into the garage," Louise replied.

Terry grabbed the hammer he always kept under the bed.

"You look out of the window and tell me which way they run," Terry told Louise. Terry then ran screaming down the stairs wielding the hammer above his head, in the hope that the burglars would scarper.

Terry reached the door that connected their garage to the hallway of their house. "Can you see anyone, Louise?"

"No. Nothing."

Terry quickly opened the door and lifted the hammer above his head as he switched the light on. The garage was empty and the main 'up-and-over' garage door was closed and locked. What there was however, was several of the normally well stacked bags of coal, smashed open, with their contents scattered about the garage floor.

But then things really came to a head.

Louise walked into the kitchen as usual at seven thirty to prepare the children's breakfast. What met her was a shocking scene. Four of the kitchen cupboard doors were open. A bag of flour and a bag of sugar lay smashed and scattered about the kitchen floor. In amongst this mess lay an almost empty squeezy bottle of tomato sauce, the contents of which had been squirted all over the kitchen and was dripping like trails of blood.

The children started to enter the kitchen as Louise was cleaning up the mess.

"Mum, what's happened?"

"Who's done this?" Louise demanded to know.

Her children denied all knowledge and her youngest started to cry.

"Oh, I'm sorry darling, come here," she said to her little girl as she gave her a cuddle.

Deep inside, Louise knew that her children would not carry out such wanton destruction. She told the kids that their dad must have spilt some stuff and did not have time to clean it up before he went to work. She gave them some cereal and toast and continued to clean up the mess.

As her children dressed into their school uniforms, Louise finally finished cleaning the kitchen. The last thing she washed in the sink was her new set of knives, in their wooden block, which had splashes of tomato sauce all over it. Louise dried each knife and placed them back into their respective slots in the wooden block.

"Right kids, come on. Are you ready? Let's get in the car," and she drove the kids to school.

When she got back home, Louise went straight to the kitchen. It was spick and span just as she had left it. She breathed a huge sigh of relief and put the kettle on. As she waited for the kettle to boil, she sat down at the kitchen table and looked around the kitchen. What on earth could have caused all that mess in the kitchen this morning?

Then Louise noticed something that chilled her to the bone. There was a knife missing from the knife block! Louise knew that she had cleaned and replaced each knife back into the wooden block just before she had taken the kids to school. All the knives had been there.

That was it! There was no way that Louise was going to allow her children to stay in this house a minute longer. Not now that the ghost, for by now Louise was convinced that's what it was, had armed itself with a knife!

Louise, Terry and the kids fled the house. And again that was the end of the story for me, and for my friends that were personally involved.

However, a couple of years later, there was a knock at my front door. It was Woody.

"You won't believe who I met last night."

"Who's that mate?" I asked, as I got us both a beer from the fridge.

"You know number one, Paradise Close?"

"Yes, of course," I replied.

"Well, I met a girl last night who knows all about the place."

Woody went on to explain that he was having a drink after work with some work colleagues, when some other people came and joined them. Some of the people Woody knew and some he didn't. One of the people Woody didn't know was a very pretty young lady who was giving him a big smile.

"Hi, I'm Woody."

"Hi," the girl blushed, "I'm Claire. Is that your real name, Woody?"

"No, just my nickname, my real name is Andy. Andy Wood."

The girl's eyes opened as wide as saucers. "Really?"

"Of course. Why?"

"Have you ever owned a house in Westlake?" she asked.

"Yes, I have."

"Was it number one, Paradise Close?"

"Yes. How do you know that?"

"Oh, my God. So you are the elusive Andrew Wood."

"What do you mean?" Woody asked.

The young Claire had a ton of questions. Why had he bought, and then sold the house so quickly? Had he experienced anything unusual in the house? She then went on to explain that she worked for an estate agents.

"One day a file dropped on my desk and I realised that I had only sold that house a few months before. Once again the occupants had already moved out and the house was 'ready to go'. I went around there and was taking some fresh photos and generally checking the place out, when an old school friend came walking by."

We gave each other a big smile and a big hug and she said to me, "You are not thinking of buying that place are you?"

"No," I told her, "I work for an estate agent. Why?"

"People round here think the place is haunted."

"Haunted? Why?"

"The first people to live here, were a young couple called Graham and Charlotte. One night, during a ferocious thunderstorm, the neighbours heard a woman screaming for help. Despite the torrential rain, some of the men in the close, ran outside to see what was happening. What met them was a chilling scene. Charlotte was lying on the rain-soaked driveway of her house and Graham was repeatedly stabbing her with a large kitchen knife."

By now, Woody was captivated by what Claire was telling him.

"I checked my files," she continued, "And I discovered that nobody had ever lived in that house for more than a few months. Why did you leave it so quickly?" she asked.

"Well actually, I never even moved in. My fiancée and I split up without ever living there."

"Oh," Claire frowned. She looked like a detective whose trail had suddenly run cold. "What about the man you sold it to, what was his name now?"

"Terry Wormhold," Woody told her.

"Yes, that's it, do you know him?"

"Yes, he is my brother in law; I sold the house to my sister."

"Your sister!" the girl's eyes lit up again, "she only stayed a few months as well didn't she? What did she think of the place?"

"She reckons the place is possessed," Woody admitted and told Claire everything that his sister had told him about the house.

Claire then told Woody everything she knew about the murder in the house. Apparently the relationship between Graham and Charlotte was pretty volatile at the best of times. The police investigation concluded that the couple had started to argue in the living room, before Graham went into the kitchen and took a large kitchen knife out of its wooden block.

Woody went cold as he recalled Louise fleeing the house, saying there was a knife missing from its block.

"Charlotte then ran upstairs and locked herself in the bathroom," Claire continued, "but Graham ran across the landing and kicked the bathroom door of its hinges."

Woody stood with his mouth wide open. He replayed the scene in his mind, of Paul sitting on the toilet and the bathroom door hanging from one hinge.

"Charlotte somehow managed to get down the stairs and out onto the driveway of the house screaming for help, but Graham caught and killed her," Claire concluded.

"So, where is this Graham now?" Woody asked.

"He's in jail, but he gets out soon on good behaviour!"

"And what about the house?" Woody needed to know.

"It's up for sale again, but not with me. My boss doesn't want anything to do with the place any more. He is sick of people threatening to kill him saying that he had sold them a haunted house!"

Old Shaun and his best friend Shamus

This one really freaked me out at first, but once I was told what was happening, I felt sorrow for old Shaun and I did my best to make sure that Shaun got his food just the way he liked it.

I was about 17 or 18 when I joined a ship called the California Star. As the name suggests, we were heading for California and my new shipmates seemed like a really good bunch of lads, so I was really happy. That first night on board, I was sitting in the crew bar getting to know the other men. In the far corner of the bar was a tall refrigerator, crammed full with cans of beer and cider and Guinness.

Sitting next to the fridge was an old man and he was talking to the fridge! As I watched him talking to the fridge, he suddenly turned his head and his tired, bright red, bloodshot eyes fixed me with a terrifying stare. I quickly looked away and pretended I was listening to whoever was talking at our table. In reality I couldn't stop thinking about the old man. How did he know I was looking at him? And that look he gave me, that really freaked me out.

"Your round, Carle," said my mate Tash, who I had sailed with before on another ship.

"Sorry, what?" I said snapping out of my thoughts.

"Go and get some beers out of the fridge."

"Oh, yeah. Okay," I said and gingerly made my way over to the old man, who was talking to the fridge again. Once again his head snapped around as I approached and he fixed me with those mad red eyes again.

"Hello, mate," I stammered nervously, "you okay?"

"Aye," he said in a thick Irish accent. "Okay, yes. Okay," he said without smiling. I quickly grabbed some beers and gave him a weak smile as I virtually ran back to our table.

During the rest of the evening, I couldn't resist looking over at the old man every now and again. I noticed how he had two cans of Guinness, one unopened with an unlit cigarette placed on top of the can. He would be smoking a cigarette and drinking his Guinness from the open can. As his cigarette was burning towards the filter, he would pick up the cigarette that was placed on the unopened can and light it with the last embers of his previous cigarette. He would then take a fresh cigarette from the packet and place it on the unopened can.

This he constantly continued to do, lighting a fresh cigarette with the remains of his last one. The true definition of a chain smoker. He also did the same with his cans of Guinness. As he finished one can, he would open the can that was sitting on the table next to him. He would then replace that can with a fresh one from the fridge, placing the unlit cigarette on top of the fresh can. Several times he caught me watching him and he would fix me with that terrifying mad red eyed stare.

It was getting towards midnight and everyone was pretty drunk, most of the men started to stagger off to bed. Tash was drunkenly telling me some story that he thought was hilarious, when someone started shouting. The old man was no longer talking to the fridge, he was stood up and he was offering the fridge a fight!

"I always get the Guinness in, and you are always smoking my smokes!" the old man shouted at the fridge.

"Yeah, you tell him, Shaun," Tash laughed, "don't you take any crap off that Shamus now."

Tash looked at me with drunken blood shot eyes and that stupid grin that was permanently fixed to his face.

"Do you know him?" I asked.

"Who? Old Shaun? Yeah, I've sailed with him a few times."

"He gives me the creeps," I confided.

"Why?" Tash asked, and then with a sudden sense of realisation he burst out laughing.

"He has caught you looking at him, hasn't he?"

"Yes" I confessed, "It freaks me out how he knows that I am looking at him."

Tash leaned towards me and his silly grin got even wider. "That's because Shamus tells him!" Tash whispered.

"Who's Shamus?"

"Shamus was Shaun's best friend," Tash grinned, "they always sailed on the same ships together. One night, while they were in port somewhere, Shaun and Shamus went to the nearest pub and got drunk as usual. When they staggered back on board ship after dark, Shamus fell to his death down an open cargo hatch. No one knows for sure what happened and it was put down to being a tragic accident, but old Shaun blames himself."

"Have you not noticed the extra can of Guinness and the extra cigarette?" Tash asked me.

"Yes, I have. What's that all about?"

"They are for Shamus," Tash told me, "Old Shaun is not talking to the fridge, he is talking to Shamus! Now Shaun is drunk and thinks that Shamus is taking him for a mug, so he wants to fight him."

"Anyway, I'm off to bed," Tash laughed, "Why don't you go over and have a Guinness with Shaun and Shamus?"

"No thanks," I squirmed, "I think I am ready for bed myself!"

My Out of Body Experience

Why am I so interested in ghosts if I have never seen one? Let me tell you why? Because I've been there, very briefly, I came out of my body.

I can listen to and write about ghost stories till the cows come home. But, just like you, I and I alone have to decide whether the person is telling me the truth, or if they are just plain telling lies.

The following story I can promise you is the truth, because it happened to me. The one and only thing that has personally happened to me, which makes me so open minded to the subject of ghosts and the afterlife.

Today, there are many books available on the subject of 'Out of Body Experiences' or OBEs. Some of these books even claim to be able to teach you how to come out of your body. No I haven't read any of them; the whole thing scares me a bit to be honest. Anyway, here is what happened to me, the truth, cross my heart.

Back in 1981, I left school at age sixteen and went away to sea in the Merchant Navy. I was the 'Galley Boy'. The Galley on a ship is the kitchen so you guessed it, my job was to constantly scrub clean the big pots and pans that the chefs used. But I loved it, sailing towards America, glorious sunshine and I was getting paid for it! What a life.

One night I was sitting having a few beers in the Crew Bar.

One of the older men, the ships carpenter, asked me how I was settling in and I said I was good. He then asked me if I had ever heard of Out of Body Experiences. I said no and he proceeded to explain to me that every night, when everyone else is asleep, he comes out of his body and flies across the ocean. He told me he flies back home to England and checks on his wife and kids. Can you imagine my reaction at sixteen, straight out of school?

"Are you winding me up?"

"It is vitally important that you listen to me, Carle. I promise you I am not winding you up. It does not matter whether you believe me or not, I just need you to promise me one thing and if you break that promise, you will kill me!"

As I sat with my mouth wide open, he went on to explain.

"When I leave my body and travel home, I am still connected to my physical body by way of my 'life line'. It's kind of like an invisible rope connecting me to my body. If my physical body wakes up when I am out of it and I can't get back in time, I die".

"Oh, my God, Bob, why do you do it then? Just stay here and have a normal sleep like the rest of us".

He laughed at my innocence and then he said, "Listen, Carle, it's not as bad as it seems. If my body wakes up and I am close by, say just flying above the ship, then I can easily get back into my body in time. However, if I am far away, like when I travel home and my body wakes up, I won't be able to get back into my body in time. My life line will then be broken and I will die".

"You can fly above the ship?"

"Oh yes, I do it most nights."

"Come off it, Bob."

"I swear to you, Carle, it's true, but like I said it does not matter whether you believe me or not, just make me a promise."

"What?"

"Don't ever, ever, knock on my door or make a noise outside of my cabin in the dead of night, because like I said, if you wake me up I could die."

"Okay, I promise."

"I mean it, Carle; no drunken pranks if you are staggering back to your cabin after a skin full."

"Okay, I promise."

And with that, he never mentioned it again. I am not sure whether I believed him or not, but I would never knock on someone's door at night. So it was an easy promise to make.

So what happened to me? Well, about two years later, I was now a seasoned sailor and had been promoted to Steward. I was home on leave and was enjoying being at home with my mum and dad and two younger sisters. I was also enjoying going out with my friends, so when the shipping company telephoned to say I was to join a ship and I was going to be away for six months, I told them I didn't want the job, I quit. The shipping officer asked if I would consider joining a different ship that would mean I would only be away for six weeks, and I agreed.

The deal was to fly to Dubai and stay the night in the Dubai Metropolitan Hotel, before joining the ship the next day. We would then sail to Cape Town and pick up a cargo of Cape apples to be brought back to England. Six weeks and I would be back home with a pocket full of cash. What could go wrong?

The hotel was fantastic and the following day I was on a real high, as me and about fifteen other men joined the ship. I had met most of the men in the hotel bar the night before and they seemed like a good bunch of lads. I felt sure we were going to have a great six weeks together. The Chief Steward wasted no time in getting all the new lads to sign the ship's articles. This is basically a contract that states you agree to join the ship 'for the duration of the voyage' and once you sign it there is no going back.

After every one had signed, we all went to our crew bar and shared a few beers, as we got to know each other. Everyone was really happy and we hadn't even finished our first beer, when the Chief Steward walked into our bar and shouted, "Can I have your attention, please. I have just been informed by head office that there has been a change of orders; the ship will sail immediately, for New Zealand!

One man jumped up and shouted, "You can't do that, I am moving house in eight weeks time, I have told my wife I will be home." Someone else shouted something similar but the Chief Steward just said, "You know the rules, you have signed the ship's articles and we go wherever head office tells us to go." With that he left the bar and left a load of men screaming and shouting. Then one of the older men announced that he had been told by head office that the ship was going to New Zealand and therefore the voyage would take five to six months. So some of us had been deliberately lied to by head office, just to get us on the ship. More screaming and shouting, but the fact was, we were stuck there with no way out.

We were told we were sailing in thirty minutes, so anyone who wants to write a letter home better be quick, no mobile phones back then. I just felt utter despair. Five minutes ago, I was the happiest man alive, now I really felt like I wanted to die. I went to my cabin and wrote a quick letter to my mum. I foolishly wrote of the utter despair I was feeling and terrified the life out of my mum by writing, "I feel like killing myself." Sorry Mum.

After handing the letter to the Chief Steward to be posted, I went back to the crew bar but the screaming and shouting was as bad as ever. I needed to be on my own and went back to my cabin, where I locked the door and lay down on my bed. I lay facing the door and curled into a ball as I closed my eyes. I can't convey to you enough the utter despair I was feeling. How was I going to cope?

I suddenly felt a really strange sensation and opened my eyes to witness my cabin door moving downwards. I then realised that my door was not moving downwards, it was me that was floating up to the ceiling! I quickly reached the ceiling and then just stayed there. It was like when you let a helium balloon loose in a room and it reaches the ceiling, then stops. I was still in a curled up position just like my physical body was on the bed, but now the light fitting was right in front of my face. I could clearly see, right in front of my eyes, that someone had painted a plastic light fitting and now the paint was peeling off. That may seem insignificant but it is proof of my experience, as I'll explain later.

Let me say, I did not feel scared at all, I felt great apart from thinking, "Oh my God, am I dead?" I starting thinking of how I could have died, I was so young. And then I thought, "Oh God it must be drugs, you have overdosed you idiot. What are they going to tell my mum? Sorry, Mrs O'Hare, it was drugs, Oh the shame of it." This was a really strange thought because the only drug I had ever tried was a cannabis cigarette.

Then I thought of old Bob and his out of body experiences. Maybe I was having an OBE. If I was, I had heard that you could float through walls, so I tried to will myself towards the wall but I couldn't move an inch. From my position on the ceiling, I could clearly see the top of my built-in wardrobe; obviously if I was standing on the floor I would not be able to see this. The top of the wardrobe was covered with dust and bits of rolled up paper. It is an unwritten law at sea that you should leave your cabin spotlessly clean for the next man and I thought what a scruffy liberty.

Then another thought occurred to me. They say that when you are having an OBE you can see yourself. I was facing the door, so I could not see myself on the bed beneath me and I couldn't move a muscle. I used all of my mental strength in an attempt to turn my head and slowly but surely my desk started to come into view. I was just getting to the point where I was about to see myself when BANG!

It was the fastest thing I have ever experienced in my life. I literally exploded back into my body and sat bolt upright in bed, covered in sweat and gasping for breath. It was like I hadn't breathed for the last five minutes. I wiped the sweat from my face with the pillow and lay back staring at the ceiling, trying to take it all in. What the hell just happened to me?

I ran everything over in my mind. The thought that I had taken drugs was laughable and then I remembered the flaking paint on the light fitting and the dust and bits of rolled up paper on top of the wardrobe. I jumped up from the bed and stood on my chair. It was exactly as I had seen it, flaking paint on the light fitting and the dust and paper balls on the wardrobe top. Impossible to see from the floor and I had only been on the ship for two minutes, it's not like I would have had time to see these things before. This for me was proof that I really was up on that ceiling and did not 'fall asleep and dream the whole thing' as has been suggested. Just for the record, I was not asleep and I was definitely not dreaming.

So why did I have an OBE and at that particular time? From what I have learned on the subject since, there are people like old Bob the ship's carpenter, who know how to come out of their body at will. However the vast majority of people have only experienced an OBE once, usually during a time of great stress or pain. Many people who have recovered from a serious car crash, have reported coming out of their bodies and watching themselves as paramedics battled to save them.

My old mate Jeff told me he had never seen a ghost; however he had an experience when he was just seven years old that he can't explain. He clearly remembers being up on the ceiling in a hospital ward, watching as he slept in bed and his mother and a doctor discussed his condition.

I believe I had an OBE that day because of the pain, the utter despair that I was feeling. I feel that some supreme being, maybe God if you believe in such a thing, decided to just take me out of myself for a little while. Just long enough to calm me down and stop me doing anything stupid.

One of my customers in my taxi is a top surgeon. We somehow got onto the subject of OBEs one day and I told him what happened to me. "Yes," he said, "that is a classic OBE, floating up to the ceiling. We have done experiments on it."

"What sort of experiments?"

"When my colleagues and I were talking to patients after an operation, some of them reported watching the whole operation from the ceiling. They were able to describe intricate parts of the operation that astounded us. We had read about experiments on the subject in a medical journal and decided to conduct our own.

At home I found a little old Dinky toy in a box of my childhood things, it was a little red tractor and when I showed it to my colleagues they all agreed it was perfect.

We placed the little red tractor on top of a stainless steel cabinet in the corner of the operating theatre. You could not see the tractor from floor level and only my colleagues and I knew it was there. And so we waited for the next patient to tell us they had floated up to the ceiling. It didn't take long. I was doing my rounds and I was asking my patient how she was feeling after yesterday's surgery."

She said, "I can't thank you enough for the hours of dedication you put in to saving my life, I watched the whole thing from the ceiling."

The surgeon sat down on the edge of the bed and asked her to describe what she had seen of the operation. He asked where she was as she watched all this and she said she was floating on the ceiling in the corner.

"Which corner?"

"The one by the door."

"What is below you, slightly to your right?"

"A steel cabinet of some kind."

"Is there anything on top of the cabinet?"

"Yes, something really odd."

"What?"

"A little red tractor toy."

The Spaceship

Not a ghost story as such this one, but I believe it to be true. And it should be of interest to you 'Trekkies' out there.

When I was seventeen, I was away at sea, working in the Merchant Navy. One evening, I was sitting in the crew bar having a few beers with John. John was about 40 years old and was married with children. He was a very level headed type of person and did not strike me as the type to make up silly stories. He was also the type of person who would not talk rubbish, without actually witnessing the incident for himself.

The subject of UFOs cropped up and I said I was not sure whether I believed in them.

"Oh, they are real, all right," John said, "I have seen one."

"Yeah right, with little green men?" I laughed.

As I said, John didn't talk rubbish and he fixed me with a very steely look.

"No. I didn't see any little green men and if you don't want to hear a true story, then let's just forget it."

"Sorry, mate," I said, "come on, don't get the hump, of course I want to hear what happened. Here, let me get us both a fresh beer and then you can tell me all about it."

And so, with a fresh can of lager in front of him paid for by me, he let me off the hook and told me this amazing story.

He was working on a ship called the Southland Star and the ship was deep in the middle of the Pacific Ocean heading for New Zealand. It was 'Movie Night' in the crew bar and this was a big event in the life of a deep sea seaman. This was the early 1970s and even VHS video recorders had not been invented yet, satellite TV was unheard of. Watching a movie involved using an old projector and reel to reel film, with a white bed sheet pinned to the wall as a screen. It was the only visual on-screen entertainment the sailors had and most of the crew would be in the bar for movie night.

John told me; "We were half way through the movie and it was just getting to a really good bit, when suddenly someone turned all the lights on and turned the projector off. There were the usual cries of, "hey what's going on?" and everyone turned to look at Tommy, who had just turned the projector off. Tommy was on his first trip as a proper Able Bodied Seaman. He was not just a deck boy or a junior seaman any more, he was a proper AB and he had responsibilities, he was on watch.

"You better come out and see this, lads," he announced, "There is a spaceship floating above the ship!"

"You have been smoking too much of that weed," the old boson shouted and all the men laughed.

"I am not kidding you," Tommy said, "They have even got the captain out of his bed. He is on the wing of the bridge

47

watching this, all the officers are watching."

This news, of course, grabbed every one's attention and everybody filed out the door onto the deck, including my storyteller John.

"We all walked out onto the deck and looked at the sky. As usual the stars were magnificent and it was a beautiful, warm, clear night. And there was definitely no flying spaceship."

"You lying little git, Tommy," the men chastised him, "Is this your idea of a joke because you are on watch and missing the movie?"

Tommy just smiled at the men. "You just watch this," he said.

Suddenly, a bright light lit up the horizon in the east and within a split second the blinding light had flashed across the sky and then stopped dead! Right above the ship. The men gasped in astonishment and one or two of them even ran back indoors.

"Why? What was there?" I asked John.

"Just like you see in the magazines," John told me, "A huge rotating silver disk, with the most amazing display of lights underneath it. It just hung there in the sky, absolutely silent."

"Watch this," said Tommy, "It will shoot off north and disappear over the horizon, before coming back from the east again."

Sure enough the men watched as the space ship flashed across the sky and disappeared over the horizon, only for it to return a few minutes later. Eventually the space ship flashed away and did not come back.

I still don't know what to make of this story, but like I said, John didn't strike me as a liar and he assured me that the captain entered the incident in the ship's log.

"I was on watch the next day," John continued, "when the captain came over and started chatting to me. I asked him what he thought about the spaceship."

"I have no idea," the captain replied, "You saw as much as I did and I have never seen anything like that before."

"Did you write it into the ship's log?" John asked.

"Of course," the Captain replied, "and I have sent a telegram to Head Office. It is up to Head Office to decide what to make of it now."

Summerdale

As I have already mentioned, these stories are to be a mix of what my friends have told me and strange things that I have experienced myself. Therefore, I feel it most appropriate to now move onto the collective stories of 'Summerdale'.

In 1988 I arrived back home in Liverpool, having spent the best part of the last decade travelling the world in the Merchant Navy. Living back in my father's house was okay, but not ideal. I soon hooked up with my two best friends, Paul and Woody. Woody was now a fitter down the coal mines and Paul was employed as a designer for a local furniture company. I had secured a job with a ferry company, sailing from Holyhead in Wales to Dublin in Ireland.

Paul and Woody were still living with their parents and decided to look for a flat share to rent, I half joked that if they found a decent three bedroom flat, I would move in as well.

Paul worked nine to five, so I accompanied Woody on a tour of the local estate agents. At the very first estate agent we tried, the young lad behind the desk said, "I think I might have exactly what you are looking for."

We climbed into his car and less than half a mile later we

pulled into the small, but private driveway of a huge Victorian mansion. As I stepped from the car I could see that the place had obviously been neglected for some time, but it was impressive nonetheless. There was a big main front door and a smaller door to the left, with a walled concrete stairway going up the right hand side of the building. The estate agent explained that the house was now split into four separate flats.

In the flat through the main front door lived a single bloke called Brian. Up the stairway on the right lived a young lad called Tommy, with his German girlfriend Gerta. At the back of the house, in the garden or basement flat, lived an old lady called Alice, who had lived there for decades.

The vacant flat he then showed me and Woody was through the smaller door to the left, which he bluntly pointed out was, "Apparently the servants' quarters in the old days," as if that didn't matter. It mattered to me; I couldn't wait to get in the place. The moment I walked through the door and first set eyes upon the old oak carved staircase snaking its way upstairs, I was amazed. I knew this was a hidden gem.

Judging by the huge cobwebs the place had obviously been empty for a long time. All I could think of is, "how much is the rent?" When we were told that if the three of us shared this three storey, three bedroom palatial pad, the rent would only be ten pound a week each, and if we cleaned the place up, the landlord would be willing to waive the first few weeks rent, we immediately signed the tenancy agreement and moved in.

The flat consisted of, on the ground floor, the entrance

hall with its old full length mirror still attached to the wall, where, "One may check one's attire before venturing outdoors." There was a large living room with its windows overlooking the garden and a kitchen, small but big enough for us and presumably big enough for the servants. Up the snaking old oak stairs to the first floor, there was a bathroom and a large bedroom, overlooking the garden, which Paul claimed. Up the snaking old staircase again to the top floor, were two more bedrooms, one large bedroom overlooking the garden at the back of the house and a small bedroom with a small arched window facing the front of the property. Woody wanted the big bedroom and I said I was happy to take the small bedroom, although the window did remind me of the Amityville horror.

And so we settled in and while Paul and Woody seemed quite happy to retire to their respective bedrooms at night, I never quite liked the look of my room after dark and chose to sleep on the settee in front of the fire instead. Paul and Woody stayed in the house every night. Sometimes their girlfriends would also stay over. I would be away for several days at a time working on the ferry, however, when I did come home, the pair of them would tell me strange stories.

Apparently no matter how many times they changed the light bulb on the top floor, it would keep blowing. Okay, we put this down to the dodgy old electrics in the house. However, it still meant that if Woody wanted to use the toilet at night, he would need to descend the stairs in the dark. One night he did and as he was making his way up the dark stairway to his room, he suddenly froze on the stairs. Although it was pitch black someone, or something, that Woody described as 'blacker than black' was blocking his way on the stairs. As quickly as he thought he had seen it, it disappeared and Woody ran into his room and jumped into bed, trying to convince himself that he was seeing things.

Several nights later, both Paul and Woody had their girlfriends stay over and after they had all gone to bed, Woody's girlfriend Annette went down the stairs in the dark to use the toilet. Woody heard Annette flush the toilet and as she started to climb the stairs in the dark, she screamed.

This not only brought Woody running from his upstairs bedroom, it also brought Paul and his girlfriend Leslie out onto the landing. Woody took Annette in his arms as she told him she thought she saw someone on the stairs, but then whoever it was disappeared. Woody tried to reassure his girlfriend by admitting that he had also seen it, then they all looked at Leslie in amazement, as she whispered, "I've seen it as well, twice!"

Who, or what scared the three of them on the stairs, we can only hazard a guess, but what Woody saw several weeks later may well hold the answer.

Woody was always a keen motorbike fan and one Sunday afternoon he was stood in front of the old full length mirror in the entrance hall, fastening up his leather biker's jacket, in eager anticipation of taking his bike for a spin. He checked his appearance in the mirror and smiled to himself, "Boy, you are looking good," he thought and he pulled his crash helmet over his head.

As the crash helmet came down over his eyes and settled into position on his head, Woody froze and his heart and his breathing seemed to stop. Through the refection in the old mirror, Woody could clearly see a young lad of about fourteen years of age standing on the bottom step of the stairs, watching him!

Woody takes up the story.

"I was more amazed than scared and although the boy looked as solid as you or me, I guessed he must be a ghost because he was dressed in Victorian clothes that looked like his Sunday best. My automatic instincts told me to turn and look directly at him, but I just knew that if I looked away from the mirror he wouldn't be there. I really wanted to speak to him, so I said, "Hello."

The boy didn't respond and for a few tense moments he and Woody continued to look at each other via the reflection of the old mirror.

"What's your name?" Woody asked.

The boy rested his elbow on the carved oak stair rail but still refused to speak. "Did you live here before me?" Woody asked, again the boy refused to answer.

"Okay." Woody said, "I am going to look away from the mirror and turn to face you. Please do me a favour and don't disappear, I only want to speak to you." Again the boy did not respond, so Woody slowly turned his head to face him, but there was nobody there!

Woody quickly looked back to the mirror, but the boy was

gone. "Please come back," Woody shouted, "I just want to talk to you," but the big old house was silent and empty. Suddenly feeling a bit scared, Woody decided to forget the bike ride and went to the pub for a few stiff drinks instead.

So that's what my friends told me happened to them in the big old house that we shared called Summerdale.

Although I never saw any ghosts myself, something happened to me in the house one day that I am convinced was something supernatural wanting to help me.

I came home from working on the ferry one afternoon and stepped into the entrance hall of the old place. "Hello," I shouted, "Is anyone home?" Only the silent stillness of this grand old residence answered me, so I cracked open a can of beer and flicked the TV on. I was kind of half sitting half slouching on the settee, with my beer in my left hand and my right arm resting on the arm of the settee.

Then something happened that frightened the life out of me. My right arm started to move backwards and forwards of its own accord, rubbing on the arm of the settee. I jumped out of my skin, dropping the beer on the floor. I grabbed hold of my arm but now it just felt like normal. Trying to rationalise what had just happened, I convinced myself that I must have trapped a nerve in my arm because of the way I was sitting.

"That's all it was," I told myself, "Just a trapped nerve."

I cleaned up the spilt beer and got a fresh one from the fridge. Within seconds of sitting back down on the settee, my arm started moving on its own again. I jumped to my feet and stared at the settee. That was no trapped nerve, something was moving my arm.

Suddenly a 'message' came into my mind. There was no voice, just a telepathic message that simply said, "Your bracelet."

My Mum had not long died and I had been deeply upset to have lost the gold bracelet she had given to me for my twenty-first birthday. I just knew that the ghost, or whatever it was that was moving my arm, was telling me that my bracelet was inside the settee. Sure enough when I searched down the back of the settee, I found my bracelet. I always slept on the settee and it must have slipped off my wrist as I slept.

Was it just coincidence, or did some supernatural influence help me out that day? As I sat down and slipped my bracelet back over my wrist, I nearly shouted, "Thank you." I quickly decided against it however, just in case I heard a disembodied voice say, "You're welcome!"

Old Jeff's House

Many years ago, I had the great pleasure to meet an old man called Jeff. Jeff and I became great friends and I would often go to his house and watch the football with him and his other friends. Sadly he is no longer with us.

Jeff lived alone in a big old house which he told me, according to the deeds, was once an old coaching house, where people would park up their horse and carriage and stay for the night.

On one of the first occasions I visited Jeff's house, he opened a door and showed me a flight of steps leading down into a cellar.

"Can I have a look?" I asked him.

"Of course you can. Come on, I'll come with you," and with that he led me down the stairs.

"Look at this," he said, "what do you think that is?"

"It looks like a bricked up window," I replied.

"Yeah, I think so too," he said. "There is another one over there."

"Why would you have windows underground?" I asked him.

"Exactly," said Jeff, "You wouldn't, which leads me to the conclusion that this cellar must have been the original cottage. Then, sometime later, they have raised the ground level and built the new house on top of the old one, utilising this as a cellar."

"How interesting. Jeff?" I asked, "Have you ever seen any ghosts?"

"No," he laughed. "There are no ghosts in this house, none that I have seen anyway."

"Have you ever seen a ghost?" I asked.

"No," he said, "I had an out of body experience when I was sick in hospital as a child."

"Really? What happened?"

"Nothing much, I just remember that I was up on the ceiling in the top corner of the room, just floating there. Below me I could see myself asleep in the bed and my mum talking to a doctor."

"I believe you," I told him. "I have had a similar experience myself."

Although Jeff had never seen a ghost, he told me of a very interesting little tale th

Trungpa

In 1967, Jeff was 26 years old and was a bit of a "hippy" or "beatnik". He was living in a squat in London and in his never ending search for his next meal he discovered a Tibetan Buddhist walk-in centre. Jeff found the Tibetans to be extremely nice people, who would give anyone a free meal and in return Jeff volunteered to help cook the food in the kitchen.

Jeff struck up a particular friendship with the young Buddhist monk in charge of the centre, whose name was Trungpa.

One day Trungpa announced to Jeff that the Buddhists had bought a big old house with several acres of land in Scotland, near Lockerbie. A team of Buddhists, including Trungpa, were to go and live in their new home in Scotland and turn it into a Buddhist retreat. Jeff, Trungpa announced, was to go with them as the cook.

"Oh, I don't know, ya know," said Jeff, in his thick Liverpool Scouse accent. "I'm not really a cook, ya know."

Trungpa laughed one of those huge belly laughs of his. "You very good cook," he said, in his broken English, "Yes, you come with us." It sounded more like a demand than a request and the following day Jeff found himself in a minibus with Trungpa and the other Buddhist monks, heading for Scotland.

The Tibetan Buddhists christened their new home "Samye Ling" and despite his initial misgivings, Jeff loved the place and stayed for several years.

One day, Jeff was in the kitchen preparing the evening meal, when he was surprised to see Trungpa walk in. The Buddhist monks were very religious in their time keeping and, apart from the two oldest monks who never seemed to bother with meditation, the other monks would always go to their respective rooms and meditate for two hours, between three and five o'clock.

As it was about four o'clock, Jeff wondered why Trungpa was standing in the kitchen looking at him. Jeff waited for whatever he presumed Trungpa was about to say to him, but Trungpa suddenly turned and quickly walked out of the kitchen, using the opposite door he had entered by.

Jeff thought it was very strange and just then one of the old monks walked in.

"Where is Trungpa going?" Jeff asked.

The old monk stared at Jeff. "Trungpa is in his room meditating," the old monk announced.

"No, he's not," said Jeff. "He has just walked through here."

The old monk smiled at Jeff, and Jeff thought he was being patronising.

"Don't you patronise me," said Jeff. "I know what I saw."

"Oh, I know you saw him," the monk replied, "that's why

I am smiling. He must be getting good at it!"

"Good at what?" Jeff asked.

"Trungpa," the old Monk explained, "has been practising what you would call in English 'bi-location'."

"What? You mean I didn't really see him?"

"No, you didn't," replied the monk. "What you saw was only his shade!"

Jeff shook his head and went back to peeling the vegetables, "This place gets weirder every day."

That evening, Jeff and some of the other monks were sitting in the communal room chatting and drinking tea. Jeff and Trungpa were sat at a table in the corner of the room playing chess. Jeff slipped a quarter bottle of rum from his pocket and quickly poured a tot into his tea. Jeff gave Trungpa a knowing look and Trungpa, after glancing over his shoulder at the other monks, gave Jeff a knowing look in return.

Jeff quickly poured a tot of rum into Trungpa's tea. They were not supposed to drink alcohol, but this was Jeff and Trungpa's little secret, going back to their days in London when Jeff would sneak Trungpa out to a back street pub where nobody would recognise him. It was one of the reasons he loved Jeff.

"I saw you today," Jeff whispered.

"I know you did," Trungpa smiled. "I could tell by the way you looked at me."

"Samtin told me that you were not really there, you were bi-locating."

"That's right," replied Trungpa. "That's why I left the kitchen so quickly."

"Why?" Jeff asked.

"I am only just beginning to learn how to do it," Trungpa explained. "I was afraid that if I did not get out of the kitchen quickly, I might disappear in front of you. I did not want to frighten you."

"Wow! Can you teach me?"

Trungpa gave a huge belly laugh. "Maybe one day," he promised, "In the meantime, you keep practicing your meditation!"

Footnote.

I was fortunate enough to visit Samye Ling with old Jeff and I witnessed firsthand how much he was welcomed by the Tibetan monks who live there. I have since been back with some of his other friends to leave his ashes there.

Type 'Samye Ling' into Google and take a look for yourself. Better still, go and visit this amazing place. And it is free, just like they always intended it to be.

More stories from old Jeff's house

We are going to the fair

One afternoon I called round to old Jeff's house to see how he was, as he had just been diagnosed with terminal cancer. Jeff was asleep in a special hospital bed in his living room and Hank was keeping an eye on him.

"Here," Hank gestured, "come through to the conservatory."

"I proper nearly shat myself in here today," said Hank, and straight away I knew what he was going to say. He had seen another ghost.

"What? You saw a ghost in here?"

"No, but I heard them," he replied. "I was stood right there," and he pointed to a spot by the windows.

"I was just standing there looking at the garden and the woods beyond, when I suddenly heard a girl giggle. I immediately went stone cold with fright, because obviously I knew there were no little girls in the house and there was no TV or radio turned on."

"Then the girl whispered, 'I can't wait to go to the fair!' Can you?"

"I was so scared; I could not turn around and was nervously glancing at my shoulder, when another girl said,

63

"Shush, I think he heard us!"

"That done it," Hank told me. "I turned and ran through the kitchen into the living room. If I would have seen them I would have run straight through them, I was that scared. But, thankfully, there was nobody there."

The Man

A few days before Jeff died; I called around to his house to see how he was doing. He was awake and he was propped up in his hospital bed in the living room watching TV. Hank was caring for him.

"Hello mate, how are you feeling today?" I asked.

"Not too bad thanks, Carle," he answered.

Then Hank said to Jeff, "Tell Carle what you saw today."

"Umm," Jeff mused, "strange that."

"What did you see mate?" I asked him.

"A man!"

"What man?"

"I don't know who he was, but a man walked into the living room from the hallway door. He walked right past me, without looking at me or saying anything and he walked through to the kitchen. I wandered who he was? Maybe a friend of Hank's? And I propped myself onto one elbow and looked behind me into the kitchen, to see what he was doing. And he was just standing there. Looking at me!"

"Anyway," Jeff said, as he pointed at Hank. "He'll tell you the rest. I'm missing QI on the telly here."

As Jeff went back to watching his favourite programme, Hank told me,

"I saw him propping himself up and I asked him if he needed a hand. He said no and he was staring into the kitchen. I asked him what he was looking at and he asked, 'Who's that?'"

"I asked, "Who's who?" and Jeff said, "Him! Standing there!"

Hank told me, "Carle, there was nobody there!"

"I asked Jeff how old this man was. And he said, 'erm, not as old as me, but I reckon older than you.' (Between 50 and 73)."

Jeff continued to stare at the kitchen doorway. "I've got to be honest with you, mate," Hank confessed, "I can't see anyone."

"Do you think it could be your dad?" Hank asked. (Jeff's dad died in WW2 when Jeff was only young, so he only had brief memories of his dad).

"Err, I don't think so. It doesn't look like him. He's gone now anyway," and with that Jeff picked up his TV remote and started flicking through the channels.

Hank continued to tell me, "Obviously I was scared, but I knew I was going to have to go and look eventually, so I stood up and looked into the kitchen. It was empty! I walked through to the conservatory and it too was empty. And the door was locked!"

When you're dead, you're dead.

Only once, in my fifty years of life on this planet, have I personally witnessed something that I am at a dead loss to explain. I can only conclude that it must have been the actions of a ghost, possibly my old mate Jeff.

Jeff died on the 28 of December, my birthday. A week later, I and several of his other friends carried his coffin into the crematorium. After the service, we all went back to old Jeff's big old house. While all the other mourners were indoors chatting, I sat alone in the garden with a can of beer and began to cry as I reminisced.

I looked to the sky and I asked Jeff to give me a sign that he was still about. "Even appear at the bottom of the garden and give me a wave!" but of course nothing happened. I dried my eyes and went indoors to get a fresh beer. I grabbed a beer from the fridge and five men were stood in a circle in the kitchen, drinking cans of beer and talking, so I joined them.

The topic of conversation was ghosts and the afterlife. One of the men, called Ray, is a master poacher and has killed thousands of animals for food, from rabbits to deer.

"It's all a load of rubbish!" Ray announced, "When you're dead, you're dead. I should know, I have killed enough things."

Suddenly something flew off the kitchen shelf and hit Ray

in the head! We all gasped and Hank bent down and picked up the missile.

When old Jeff was alive, we would sometimes order a Chinese takeaway. After the meal, old Jeff would always wash and dry the plastic containers that the food came in, along with their lids. Then he would put them on the kitchen shelf. One day I asked him, "what are you keeping those for?"

"They might come in handy one day," was his reply and I shook my head thinking, "how old school is that?"

Now for some inexplicable reason, one of the plastic lids had flown off the shelf and hit Ray in the head. The kitchen is enclosed in the house; no wind could have blown that plastic lid off that shelf. And believe me, if you would have witnessed it for yourself, you would agree that the plastic lid flew through the air like a frisbee!

Of course, Ray was not hurt and we all laughed it off. I turned around and my wife Elaine was standing in the kitchen doorway. She is the biggest sceptic in the world.

"Did you see that?" I asked her.

"Yeah," she replied, "I have got to admit, I can't explain that one."

Footnote

I told the previous story to my mechanic Joe, as he was fixing my car. "It's funny you should mention that," he said, "I was at a funeral once, and when we all went back to the home of the deceased, all the men were sitting around the kitchen table drinking beer. As men do, there was a few swear words and lurid stories and dirty jokes being bandied around as the men laughed."

The lady of the house, whose husband was the deceased, said, "Oooh, if he could hear you lot now. You know he would have joined in any banter with you lot down at the pub, but you know, he didn't like any swearing in front of the ladies."

"Then with impeccable timing," my mechanic continued, "a framed photograph of the deceased fell off the wall and smashed!"

"See, I told you," his wife said, "been on that wall for years that photograph has. Why would it fall off now?"

The Bargain Booze Ghost

Why is it that some people apparently see a ghost, when others don't? This is a very strange tale of a ghost that apparently walked straight through me and yet I never saw or felt a thing. My friend Richard tells me he has caught glimpses of ghosts all his life and I personally witnessed this event, which was amazingly backed up by another sighting of the ghost several weeks later.

One evening, my mate Richard and I walked into our local off licence to buy some beers. The football was on TV and we were keen to grab our beers quickly and get back home in time to catch the start of the match. We grabbed our beers from the fridge and I walked over to the till and handed my money to the young long-haired lad who worked in the shop. He reminded me of maybe a student, who was earning some part-time money.

He gave me my change and I looked at Richard standing next to me, but he was looking at the display of chocolate bars in front of the till, deciding which ones to buy. In that split second I remember thinking, "should I wait for him or wait in the car?" As I was driving and probably in an attempt to get him to hurry up in case we missed the start of the football, I decided to wait in the car and left the shop.

The shop was very modern with the whole frontage being mostly glass, with strong neon lights lighting up the interior. From where I was sitting in the car with my driver's window down, I had a clear view of what was happening in the shop. There was only Richard and the young shop assistant in the shop and Richard was talking to him and pointing to the back of the shop. I remember thinking, "Come on, Richard, hurry up, you know the football is about to start."

Then what I was witnessing inside the shop became even more bizarre. Richard, who is six feet four, stood with his back to the entrance door of the shop, as if he wasn't going to allow anyone to enter. The young shop assistant then walked to the back of the shop and walked through an open doorway that led to a small storeroom. The long-haired lad then walked back into the shop and shrugged his shoulders at Richard. The pair of them continued to talk some more, leaving me wondering, "What the hell are they doing?"

Eventually, Richard came out of the shop and as he walked towards me he said, "You have just missed a ghost, in fact it may have walked right through you!"

As we drove back home Richard told me what happened. Apparently, as I left the shop a man walked in. Richard never bothered to look at him directly, he just caught a glimpse of him as he walked behind Richard and headed for the wine display on the back wall of the shop. Richard also caught a glimpse of the man's shirt, blue and white stripes. Richard and the young lad on the till then both heard a crashing sound come from the storeroom at the back of the shop. It sounded like someone had walked into a stack of plastic crates containing bottles, only without actually knocking them over.

"What was that?" the young lad asked.

"It must be that fella," Richard replied.

"What fella?"

"The one that's just come in."

"I never saw any fella."

"Well, I did," Richard replied, "He headed straight for the wine display, he must have gone in the storeroom."

"What shall I do?"

"Go and have a look," said Richard.

"I'm not supposed to leave the till."

"Don't worry," Richard promised, "I won't let anyone in, you go and stick your head round the storeroom door."

The young lad poked his head around the open door way of the storeroom, but there was nobody there. There was however, several stacks of plastic crates containing bottles of beer in the middle of the room, and one of the stacks looked as though it had been knocked out of its usual square position by a couple of inches. As if someone had walked into it, maybe?

The young lad came back out of the storeroom and shrugged his shoulders at Richard, "There is nobody there."

"Well, you heard that crashing sound didn't you?" Richard asked.

"Oh yeah," the young lad replied, "and it does look like someone has walked into a stack of crates in there."

"Well, I saw a man walk in here with a blue and white striped shirt on," Richard told him and with that he left the shop and approached me in the car.

Interesting little tale and that should be the end of the story, except things took an unexpected twist. I walked into the same off licence the following night and the same young lad was at the till. After I explained who I was from the night before, I asked him his version of events and he confirmed exactly what Richard had said.

A couple of weeks later, I walked into the off licence and the same young lad was tapping away at his till. The shop was quite busy with a small queue waiting to be served at the till. The young lad glanced up at me as I entered the shop and when he realised it was me his eyes lit up.

"I've seen it!" he almost shouted, "same blue and white striped shirt."

"You're kidding me?"

"No, I swear, wait till I serve these customers and I'll tell you."

So, when the shop was empty he told me.

"The other night, I had a young trainee girl working with me. I was dying for a ciggie, so as soon as the shop was empty, I told the trainee girl I was just going to have a sly smoke in the storeroom. I promised her that I would be keeping an eye on her from the storeroom doorway and I would save her half of the cigarette. Standing just inside the storeroom doorway, I watched as a woman came in and bought some cigarettes. The young girl served her without a problem and as the woman left the shop a man walked in and he headed straight for the wine display on the back wall. Because I was standing just inside the storeroom doorway, I could no longer see him and I just presumed he was looking at the wines."

"Then the young trainee girl comes over and says, "Are you giving me some of that ciggie then?"

"Yes," I told her, "but you better serve that man first."

"What man?" she asked.

"So I looked around the doorway," my long-haired storyteller told me, "and I swear to you mate, there was nobody there and yet I saw him come in."

"And do you know what, mate?" he continued, "It never occurred to me at the time; the bloke was wearing a blue and white striped shirt."

The Club Steward

This is another tale told to me by my friend Hank, who claims to be able to see, or sometimes only hear ghosts. I must point out that Hank is not pleased with his apparent talent and wishes he didn't see ghosts, as sometimes they put the right willies up him. Like the time when he was a boy and the father of one of his friends died. The day after the untimely death of this man, Hank called round to his friend's house and was invited into the living room. The dead man's family and friends were all sitting drinking tea and reminiscing what a great man he was. No one would sit in the armchair by the fire, as this was the deceased's favourite chair. It's a good job too, because Hank could plainly see the dead man sitting in his chair and further more he was smiling at Hank as if to say, "You can see me, can't you?"

Anyway, the club steward.

In the 1970s, Britain was dotted with what were then called 'Labour clubs' or 'Working Men's clubs'. The few that remain open today, tend to be called 'Social Clubs'. The landlord of these Labour clubs was known as The Club Steward. Hank was nineteen and had just started courting Melony, or Mel as she preferred to be called. Hank took Mel to the local Labour club for a drink and after getting them both a drink from the bar, he looked around for somewhere suitable to sit.

The club had a huge function room and a smaller room known as 'The Bar'. Only about 20 people were in the bar and the function room was closed and in darkness. In the bar was a wide staircase that led up to a smaller seating area upstairs. "Come on," Hank said to Mel, "We will sit up here; it's a bit more private."

Only three other people were in the upstairs seating area, two women, who were gossiping away and an old man sitting on his own with a pint of dark beer, either Guinness or mild, Hank guessed. Hank sat down at an empty table with Mel and nodded his head in acknowledgement to the old man, who was smiling at him from across the room.

Hank sat chatting to Mel and a little while later the young club steward came to the top of the stairs and shouted, "Last orders at the bar, folks, and would the last one down turn the lights off for me, please," as he pointed to a light switch on the wall. The two women immediately got up and followed the steward down the stairs. Hank asked Mel if she wanted another drink and she said no. "Let's just finish these and go home."

Hank agreed and a little while later he and Mel finished their drinks and walked to the top of the stairs, leaving the old man sitting by himself, who was still unnervingly smiling at Hank.

"Don't forget to turn the lights out," Mel said.

"He'll do it," Hank replied

"Who?"

"Him," Hank said, and he nodded his head in the direction of the old man. "You'll turn the lights off, won't you, mate?" Hank asked the old man. The old man continued to smile at Hank, as he slowly nodded his head.

Hank turned back to Mel who was stood staring at him, open mouthed.

"What?" Hank asked.

"I can't see anyone!"

Hank swung his head back to the old man, who was still sitting there smiling at Hank and with a sense of mounting dread, Hank realised that once again he was staring at a ghost. Hank took hold of Mel's elbow and ushered her down the stairs, "Come on," he said, "Let's go."

As Hank and Mel left the bar, Hank said to the young steward, "I haven't turned the lights out, mate, I don't know if there is an old man sitting up there or not?" The young steward gave Hank a quizzical look, either there was an old man up there or there wasn't? But Hank didn't hang around to explain.

A few days later Hank called into the club again, to have a drink with his dad who as Hank's mum would say, "Virtually lives in the place." Hank bought a pint of lager and joined his dad at a table. Hank noticed an old lady sitting alone at another table and she smiled at him, then she walked over and joined Hank and his dad at their table.

"You've seen him haven't you?" the old lady asked Hank.

"Who?" Hank asked.

"The steward told me that you came in here with your girl the other night and you told him you didn't know whether there was an old man upstairs or not."

"That's right," Hank replied.

"What did he look like? What was he wearing?" the old lady wanted to know.

Hank gave her a brief description of the old man and told her that he was wearing a brown corduroy suit.

"You know who you have seen, don't you?" the old lady asked, and without waiting for a reply she called the young steward over to their table. "It was definitely him," the old lady told the young steward, "Same brown corduroy suit."

The steward sat down with them and Hank's dad sat with a bemused look on his face, as he never had a clue what they were talking about. The steward asked Hank again to describe the old man he had seen upstairs and what he was wearing.

"Did he have a drink?" the young steward asked.

"Yes, it was a pint of either Guinness or mild," Hank told him.

"Guinness," was the steward's reply, "It was Guinness."

The steward looked at the old lady and she said, "I told ya."

"Would one of you two mind telling me what's going on?" Hank asked. The young steward looked at Hank and said,

"I think you saw my dad. He was the club steward here for years, but he died seven years ago."

The old lady then told Hank that she had seen the old club steward too, but she didn't know who he was until she talked to the young steward about it. She told Hank that she was sitting upstairs with her husband, playing bingo. The place was busy because it was bingo night and as she was checking her numbers, she glanced up at an old bloke in a brown corduroy suit, who had suddenly joined them at their table.

He smiled warmly at her and she smiled back, then she went back to checking her numbers. She never thought it was strange that the old man had sat opposite her, as the place was busy and he had to sit somewhere. However when someone called, 'House' and the game was stopped, she turned to her husband and said, "I only needed one then." Her husband just nodded as he had no interest in the bingo whatsoever, and by now the lady was starting to get a bit creeped out by the man sitting opposite, who was still smiling at her.

The bingo caller started calling the new set of numbers and she tried to concentrate on the game and ignore the man. However when someone called, 'House' and stopped the game, she decided she had had enough. She punched her husband in the leg and said to him, "Will you tell him to stop staring at me?"

"Who?" her husband asked.

"Him!" she demanded and nodded to what her husband could only see as an empty chair.

"What the hell are you talking about, woman?" her husband grunted.

"And then," the old lady continued, "I swear, he faded away right before my very eyes!"

The young steward showed Hank a photograph of his dad and Hank had to agree that it was probably him. So maybe the old club steward is still enjoying his pint of Guinness and still sitting and smiling with his customers.

Taxi drivers' tales

I work as a taxi driver and if my customer is the talkative type, I often ask them if they have ever seen a ghost?

Here are a few tales that my customers have told me so far and I promise to bring you more.

Granddad's bell

My passenger was a young girl aged about twenty. She was chatting along merrily to me and I took the opportunity to ask my favourite question.

"Have you ever seen a ghost?"

As so often happens when I ask this question, the immediate answer is usually no. And then people add, "But a strange thing happened a couple of years ago, though."

"Why? What happened?" I asked her.

"When my granddad was sick before he died, he was virtually bedridden in his bedroom up stairs. He had his books and a TV and if he needed anything, he would ring a little bell and my grandma would go to see what he needed. It must have been a good twelve months after grandpa had died, when I went to visit my Grandma."

"Grandma and I were sitting having a cup of tea and a chat, when I could swear I heard granddad's bell ringing.

Only very faintly, but I could swear I was hearing it. Grandma was just chatting away to me as if nothing was happening and in the end I had to ask her.

"Grandma, what's that noise?"

"What noise dear?"

"It sounds like granddad's bell."

"You can hear that?" her grandma asked.

"Then," the girl continued to tell me, "My grandma stood up and walked to the bottom of the stairs."

"Billy, will you pack it in with that bloody bell!" her grandma shouted up the stairs, "Even Victoria is hearing it now."

Victoria told me that the bell stopped ringing and her grandma sat down again and said, "Sorry about that, dear, it's just your granddad letting me know that he is still around. Now, what were we talking about?"

The girl in the yard

I picked up a lady aged around forty. As we drove along, I noticed a group of people dressed as zombies having a drink outside a pub.

"It's not Halloween today, is it?" I asked her.

"No. Why?" she asked, "Do I look like a witch?"

I laughed and said, "No, sorry, it's just that I saw those people in fancy dress."

As we were on the subject, I took the opportunity to throw in my question.

"Have you ever seen a ghost?"

Again her immediate answer was no, but then she added, "Well, I don't know."

"Why? What happened?"

"I was cooking tea in the kitchen and my fourteen year old daughter was upstairs drying her hair, I could hear the hair dryer. Something caught my eye at the kitchen door that leads into the back yard. There was a young girl about the same age as my daughter standing in the yard, and she smiled and waved at me through the glass in the back door."

"I presumed it was a friend of my daughters and I smiled

back and moved towards the door to let her in. As I walked towards the door, I glanced at the pans of food that were cooking on the stove and when I looked back at the door, there was nobody there!"

"I opened the door and went out into the yard, but there was nobody there. And in any case the back gate was locked, so how could anyone have entered the yard?"

"So you think it was a ghost then?" I asked her.

"Well, I don't know," she replied, "I do know I definitely saw her and then she was gone, so what else would you call it?"

Good point!

The ghost and the bath taps

Only recently I went to an address in my taxi and four young girls in their early twenties climbed into my car. The young girl who sat in the front with me was very chatty and asked me my name and what my interests were? I told her I was trying to write a book.

"Really?" she asked, "What is it about?"

"It's a collection of ghost stories," I told her, and then of course I threw in my question, "Have you ever seen a ghost?"

She laughed and turned to her three friends who were taking selfies of themselves on their phones.

"Hey girls! Have you heard this? Carle, our driver here, wants to know if I have ever seen a ghost."

"Just go in her house, mate," said one of the girls in the back of the car, and then she went back to taking photographs on her phone.

I turned my attention back to my new-found friend sitting next to me.

"You have a ghost in your house?" I asked her.

"Have I ever! The bloody thing has flooded my house out twice. It seems to have a fascination with my bath taps. The thing is I am paranoid about spiders coming up out of the plug hole, so I used to leave the plug in its hole. However, I can't do that anymore because the ghost turns the taps on and floods the house."

I must point out to you, dear reader, that I was a bit sceptical, but then she went on to tell me two more fascinating incidents and one of her friends in the rear of the car backed up her story.

"Hey, Joanne, tell Carle what happened with the bath taps."

"Three times I watched them taps turn themselves off, mate," said one of the girls in the back of the car, but she was too interested in her phone to elaborate. I turned my attention back to my storyteller.

"So she has seen it as well?"

"Yes," the girl told me, "Don't get me wrong, none of us has actually seen this ghost, but it seems to be most active when I am getting ready to go on a night out. I have arguments with it."

"Why? What happens?"

"The four of us were going on a night out," she continued, "Joanne arrived early at my house and I said, "I haven't even had a bath yet," and Joanne said, "Well, hurry up."

"I put the plug in the bath and turned the taps on, but the ghost immediately turned them off again. 'Stop it!' I shouted, 'I am late enough as it is,' and I turned the taps back on. As soon as the water started to flow, the taps turned themselves off again. 'Oh, please, not tonight,' I begged but as soon as I turned the taps back on, the ghost turned them off again. Then it dawned on me. None of my friends had actually seen this and I was not sure whether they believed me or not when I told them about it, so I shouted Joanne."

"Joanne! Come and see this."

"I did not know whether the ghost would do it with someone else watching, but as soon as I turned the taps on, they turned themselves off again."

"Woh! How did you do that?"

"It wasn't me, it was the ghost. Now do you believe me?"

"Do it again," Joanne demanded and twice more she watched in amazement as the taps were turned on, only to witness them turn themselves off again. Eventually the ghost decided to give up on its little game and let the water flow.

But the scariest incident she saved till last. The ghost could have burned the house down never mind flood it.

"One night, I was in the living room watching TV, when I heard a bump on the ceiling above me. I muted the TV and sure enough I could hear noises coming from the main bedroom above me. The main bedroom is full of boxes of my junk and I gingerly opened the door and looked inside. Nothing looked amiss and it was silent in the room. I was just about to close the door and dismiss it, when I caught a sweet smell of lavender. I looked again and in the centre of the room I caught sight of a little bit of smoke. I went to see what it was and there, behind some boxes, was a square purple candle, and it was lit." She explained. "It looked exactly like one of a matching pair I have in my bathroom. I went to the bathroom and sure enough, there was only one candle on the window ledge. I took both candles out into the yard and threw them in the wheelie bin."

"But you won't believe this, Carle," she continued, "When I went to the bathroom the following morning, both candles were back on the window ledge!"

"That's amazing," I told her, "Are you not scared? Don't you want to move house?"

"Well, obviously I don't want the house to go on fire, but I like it where I am and what if I move and it just follows me? I like to think it's my granddad still looking out for me."

I hope so, for her sake.

Anton

I sat there on the end of the settee with that warm feeling inside. That feeling when you know that you don't want any more to drink, but you are happy to sit and sip the last dregs of your Bacardi and coke.

It had been a great party, well, for me at least. For the three people that were still awake chatting to me however, there were mixed emotions.

My wife, Elaine, was asleep on the same settee I was sat on, with her legs across my lap. This settee was to be the bed for both of us tonight, not enough real beds to go around, so I knew then that I would be sleeping on the floor.

I was in the basement flat of a huge block of terraced houses in Earls Court Square, London SW1. No one had bothered to draw the curtains on the huge bay window and I was fascinated watching the people walk by outside, because you could only see their legs. At the party earlier, I had met a black girl who told me she was of French-African origin. She lived in one of the flats upstairs and she told me that the building we were in would have originally been built in 1873, to house rich merchant banker types. The basement flat we were standing in would have originally been the servants' quarters. Most, if not all, of the servants would have been French immigrants.

The three people that were still awake with me were my wife's Aunty June, aged about sixty, the owner of the flat and two of her three children, her eldest and only son Michael, aged about forty and her youngest daughter Victoria, aged about thirty-five.

This was the first New Year's Eve they had spent without their dad, so I sat quietly as they laughed and reminisced about what a great man he was.

"Hey, Mum, do you remember Paddy?" Victoria asked.

"Oh, that pain in the arse," June replied.

"Who's Paddy?" I asked.

"Paddy was Mick's mate," June told me, "I know it sounds like a joke, but that really was their names, Paddy and Mick. My husband Mick had a mate called Paddy. They were both so Irish that when they were drunk, which was usually most of the time, they would talk to each other and their accent was so strong that even I couldn't understand what they were talking about."

"Do you remember how Paddy used to sleep in a tomb in the graveyard?" Michael laughed.

The three of them laughed out loud, but I just stared at Michael in disbelief. "You are kidding me, right?"

"No, I swear to you," Michael said, "My dad used to bring Paddy back here after the pub. If they were quiet, my mum wouldn't wake up and Paddy would sleep on the couch. If they kept drinking however, they would usually end up arguing, sometimes even fighting."

"That's when I would get up out of bed," June continued the story. "I would throw Paddy out into the street and give Mick a whack about the head."

"If it wasn't raining or cold," Michael continued, "Paddy would sleep in the park. If it was raining, Paddy knew how to pick one of the padlocks on a tomb in the graveyard and he would sleep in there with the corpses."

"No way!" I gasped in disbelief.

I had only met these people for the first time, that morning. We had taken the children to feed the squirrels, in of all places, Brompton cemetery. I had been amazed by the place. When I had peeked through the metal grills of various tombs in the cemetery, I was shocked to see dusty old coffins hanging on the walls. I had never seen anything like that before. I always presumed that dead people were either cremated, or buried underground, not placed on a shelf for all eternity!

The thought of spending the night in such a tomb, which apparently Paddy did regularly, does not even bear thinking about.

"Hey, Mum," Michael said, "Do you remember Anton?"

"Oh, how could I forget him," June replied.

"Oh, my God, Anton!" Victoria squealed, "I had totally forgotten about him."

"Well come on, Victoria," Michael mocked, "You are thirty-five now so you can tell us the truth, Anton wasn't real was he?"

"He was real," Victoria cried, "Mum, tell him."

"Oh come on, let's go to bed, I'm sure Carle wants to go to sleep now," June yawned.

"No, I'm fine," I promised her, "I want to know who Anton is."

"Anton was Victoria's imaginary friend," Michael mocked.

"He was not imaginary," Victoria protested, "He was really there, except you couldn't see him. He told me only I could see him."

Michael howled with sarcastic laughter.

"You have to admit it, Michael, it was weird," June said, addressing her son.

"Why, June? What happened?" I needed to know.

"Well, as you may well have gathered," June replied, "if you needed Mick he would be found in the pub, usually drunk. However, he was always at home in time for the Sunday roast dinner. In his eyes, it was traditional."

The family would always sit around the old oak six-seater dining table together, for the Sunday roast. The table would normally be pushed up against the wall but on a Sunday, the table would be pulled out, just enough to allow four year old Victoria to crawl underneath and sit in one of the two chairs that were against the wall. Then dad would sit at the head of the table, with his only son, Michael, sitting at the other end. June and her eldest daughter, Sara, would then sit in the two chairs facing Victoria and the wall.

June placed the tray of roast lamb and roast potatoes on the table and everyone eagerly loaded their plate. A bowl of sprouts and a bowl of carrot and turnip, along with a large gravy boat were also brought in by June. After making sure little Victoria had what she wanted on her plate, June sat down and started to load her own.

"Mum, can Anton have some dinner?"

June looked at her little girl and then looked at her husband, who was staring back at her, without chewing the piece of lamb he had in his mouth. He had that Irish superstitious look in his eyes that June had seen many times before.

"Who's Anton, babe?"

"My friend."

"And where is Anton?"

"He's sitting here, next to me."

Michael sniggered but soon shut up, when his father's booming Irish voice bellowed across the table. "Shut up, Michael, will ya!"

"Okay," June said to her little girl, "I will get Anton a plate. What would Anton like to eat?"

The whole family then watched in amazement, as four year old Victoria spoke to the empty chair, in French!

"He said he will have meat and roasties, but not carrot and turnip, he doesn't like turnips."

"And so it continued," June told me, "Each Sunday we would sit down for our lunch and Anton would join us. Victoria would speak to him in what sounded like French, but to be honest it could have been any language, because none of us can speak French. I would get Anton a plate and Victoria would tell me what he wanted. He would never have carrot and turnip, which was surprising because Victoria loved it."

Michael started laughing again. "Hey, Mum, remember if Victoria went to the toilet, I would crawl under the table and sit in Anton's chair?"

Joan howled with laughter, "Victoria would come back in and start screaming and your dad would shout, "Michael, pack it in, will ya."

"It's not funny," Victoria screamed, "I would come back from the toilet and Anton would be standing there close to tears, because Michael was in his chair."

"So Anton was a boy, then?" I asked her.

"Well that's what's strange," she told me, "Most of the time I thought he was a boy, but sometimes he would smile or laugh in a certain way and he looked like a girl. It was like he was neither boy nor girl, if you know what I mean?"

"So what happened to him?"

"I don't know. One day he just never showed up for the Sunday roast. I remember my dad asking me, "Will Anton be wanting any dinner today?" I told him I didn't know because Anton wasn't there. I always remember what my dad said to me.

He said. "Don't worry, Princess, Anton must have found another little girl that he needs to take care of. You are getting older now, you don't need Anton anymore!"

The Bakery

As I have said, I write these stories in the belief that they are true, as it is my family and friends that have told me these tales. As in the case of my brother-in-law, Peter. Like me, Peter has never seen a ghost, but this is a story he just cannot explain.

Peter has been a plumber and gas fitter all his working life and is now approaching retirement age. Why would a man of his age and vast knowledge of life tell me lies? I don't believe he would. This is the story Peter told me.

He was working on an old bakery that was being converted into a pub. The old bloke who was employing Peter and several others, was only known as Mr Thomas. Mr Thomas was always immaculately dressed and always wore an old fashioned cravat or neck scarf. Mr Thomas was proud of his cravats, of which he had several, all of vivid blues or crimson colours.

At half past four on the dot, every afternoon, Mr Thomas would walk into the old bakery to check that the men were still at work and to check on what work had been carried out that day. Peter was working on the very top floor where the huge great mill wheel, that once ground the wheat into flour, still stood.

Mr Thomas, who Peter recalls was quite an amiable man, would often chat to Peter about how the work was progressing. Then like a typical stiff upper lip English gentleman he would say, "Very good, Peter, you carry on, old chap. I am just going to take a look at this old thing." He would then spend ages standing looking up and down and occasionally walking around, the old mill wheel. One day, Peter decided to ask him why?

"Mr Thomas?"

"Yes, old chap? What is it?"

"Why do you spend so much time looking at the old mill wheel?"

"My dear fellow," smiled Mr Thomas, "I am trying to decide what to do with it. To remove it all together would cost an absolute fortune, and why would you want to? It is part of the character of the old place. After all," continued Mr Thomas, "I do intend to call this place The Bakery, when it opens. So the question remains, how do you make a theme pub feature out of this grand old lady?" he asked, as he held both arms aloft.

Sadly, not long afterwards, Mr Thomas died peacefully in his sleep.

Mr Thomas's sons inherited his empire and instructed Peter and the other contractors to carry on as normal. About two weeks after Mr Thomas's funeral, Peter was working away in the bakery when one of Mr Thomas's sons asked him if he knew of any young labourers who might want some work cleaning the old place out.

"Sure," Peter said, "I know a young lad down at the pub

that would be happy with the money."

"Great," said Mr Thomas's son, "bring him with you tomorrow and tell him to just start cleaning from the top down."

The following morning Peter brought his young protégé to work with him and, after arming him with a yard brush, Peter took him to the top floor.

"Wow! What's that?" the young lad asked.

"It's the old mill wheel, this place used to be an old bakery. Anyway, what you have got to do is shift all this rubbish to the top of the stairs and then give the place a good brush out, got that?"

"Got it," said the young lad.

Peter then moved down the stairs to the next floor and removed two or three steps of the stairs as he needed to work on the pipe work that ran underneath the steps. After about half an hour, the young lad came to the top of the stairs and said, "Peter, you better come and talk to this inspector because I don't know what to say to him."

"What inspector?"

"The one that's up here inspecting the old mill wheel."

Peter looked about him. He was working on the stairs and nobody had passed by him. But then again, sometimes you are so engrossed in your work, it is possible that someone could have stepped over him and he never gave it a second thought. Tony the electrician was working further down the stairs.

"Tony, have you seen anyone come up the stairs?"

"No," Tony shouted back, "Why?"

"No matter," Peter shouted back and then he walked up the stairs and said to the young lad, "come and show me this inspector, then."

When Peter and his young friend walked into the room on the top floor, his young mate stood open mouthed, because there was nobody there.

"Oh, my God," says the young lad, "you think I am telling lies don't you? I swear to God, he was here. He asked me what I think could be done with the mill wheel and that's when I came and fetched you because I didn't know what to say to him."

"What did he look like?" Peter asked.

"He was an old bloke with short curly grey hair and a grey moustache, wearing a smart suit."

"Did he have anything around his neck?" Peter asked.

"Yes, it was a silky, bright blue kind of scarf thing. Why did you ask that?"

"I know it's only early," said Peter, "but the Dog and Duck opens at ten. Why don't we call it a day and go and have a pint, you are going to need one. I know I do."

The Fireman

My very good friend, Dave, is a fireman. Dave lives for his job, he absolutely loves it and would work every day if he was allowed to. Dave is so devoted to his job he is not married and lives alone in a one bed bungalow. Everything has its place in Dave's immaculately clean little dwelling and he is very analytical. He scoffs at the very notion of ghosts.

Imagine my surprise then when he called me and said, "I think there may be something in this ghost lark that you keep going on about."

"Don't tell me you have seen a ghost?"

"I don't know what to make of it," he replied, "I woke up this morning and as usual, I couldn't wait to put my uniform on and go to work. However, it was still very early, so I just lay in bed for a while gazing out of the window, watching the sunrise and listening to the birds singing."

"A movement in the corner of my room caught my eye and I turned to look. At first I thought nothing of it, but then I suddenly realised that what I was watching just wasn't possible. As usual, my fireman shirts were all washed and ironed to perfection, hanging on their hangers on my clothes rail but one of them was moving!"

"I watched in amazement as just one of the shirts slowly

turned on its swivel hanger. It turned a full 45 degree turn until it was facing me full on, then it stopped dead. I got out of bed and walked over to my shirts and stood there looking at them, trying to figure out some rational explanation."

"Then I heard a squeaking noise coming from the living room and I knew immediately what it was. My big black leather chair is mounted on a strong spring, so that it gently moves when you are sitting in it. That spring squeaks slightly and that was what I was hearing. I ran into the living room thinking I may have an intruder and watched as my empty chair rocked slightly on its squeaky spring. After two or three seconds it stopped dead."

"What do you make of that?" he asked me.

"I don't know, mate," I replied, "You tell me, you're the one who doesn't believe in ghosts."

Ha! It doesn't work

My very good friend and neighbour, Karen, told me this one. Karen and my wife Elaine are lifelong friends, as they both grew up in the same street that we all still live in. The house I now live in is my wife's childhood home. Karen's house across the road is Karen's childhood home. Her house is much older than our house, her house is an old mining 'pit house'.

Karen tells me that she has always been able to see ghosts. Ever since she can remember, she saw ghosts as a child growing up. Karen told me that she still often sees the ghosts of two women in Victorian dress, walking through her bedroom when she is in bed. The two ghosts are talking to each other but Karen can only see them, she cannot hear what they are saying. The two ghosts walk through the wall into the house next door, as if the wall is not there.

Incidentally, I am good friends with the people who live in that house next door to Karen and I will tell you a curious little tale of theirs next.

But first let's get back to Karen. I asked Karen if any of the ghosts she had seen had ever scared her.

"Only one," she said, "He was pure evil."

"Why? What happened?" I asked her.

"I managed to get Kevin (her husband) to take me to stay in one of those posh hotels for the night. You know the sort of place? Like a big old stately home that now operates as a hotel. It was £220 a night, so you can imagine what tight-arse Kevin's face was like. But I insisted I needed a break and Kevin reluctantly relented."

"The evening meal was lovely and we had a great night, having a few drinks in the lounge with the other guests, even though Kevin moaned about the prices all night. When we went up to bed, I was getting undressed, while Kevin was brushing his teeth. I pressed the switch on my old bedside lamp but it didn't come on."

"When Kevin came out of the bathroom, I told him my lamp wouldn't work and he had a quick look and said, "Oh, I don't know, could be the bulb. Do you want to get on my side?"

"No it's okay, just leave your lamp on, I will turn it out."

"Right, okay," said Kevin, and he was snoring before his head hit the pillow."

"I just lay there for a while," Karen continued to tell me, "Looking around the old room and wondering who might have lived there. Eventually, I leaned over Kevin and switched his lamp off. There was a full moon outside and shadows from the trees were dancing about the room. I lay there for a while looking at the stars through the window, thinking how magnificent they looked in the darkness of the countryside."

"I closed my eyes and started to drift into a blissfully

happy sleep, when suddenly I felt someone breathing into my face and whoever it was, their breath stank. My eyes shot wide open and the most grotesque of men was staring me straight in the face and leering at me, with the most evil grin. I tried to scream, but it just came out like a sharp intake of breath. I instinctively reached for the switch on my lamp and clicked it, but of course it didn't come on."

"Ha! It doesn't work," the grinning man sneered.

"Then the scream did come," Karen told me, "I dived out of bed and switched the main light on but of course, there was nobody there."

"What the hell?" grumbled Kevin as he woke up.

"Come on get up, we are going home," Karen announced.

"Are you nuts? Do you know how much this place has cost me? And I am drunk anyway, I can't drive."

"We are going! Get up, NOW!

And Karen did indeed make Kevin pay for a taxi to take them both home. And Kevin had to arrange for a friend to drive him back to the hotel the next day to collect his car.

The funeral director

My father's girl friend told me the following tales. Sue has been my Dad's partner for over twenty years and I know for a fact she would never lie to me.

Sue recalls her childhood as being a very happy one. Her parents would often invite their friends around to their house for the evening and Sue and her brother, Ian and sister, June, would be allowed to stay up with the adults for a while before bed, drinking Horlicks and eating toast. Sue's Dad would always tell his guests the same story. She had heard it so many times, she is convinced her Dad was telling the truth.

In the early 1930's, Sue's dad, Tommy, started courting Sue's mum, Cath. One warm summer Saturday night, Tommy took Cath to the dance. After the dance, Tommy walked his sweetheart home and they sat on the garden wall of Cath's parents, talking and laughing until gone two in the morning.

Eventually, the old wooden bedroom window above them creaked open and Cath's Dad shouted, "Are you going to sit out there all night, girl? Haven't you got a home to go to, Sunshine?"

"Whoops! I think I better be going," Tommy whispered, "I will see you tomorrow and we'll go to the park. Okay?"

"Yes, love you," Cath whispered, as she watched Tommy

walk away.

Tommy had a good five mile walk home from Prescot to St Helens and it was well after three before he reached the brow of the hill that looked down onto St Helens town centre. A sharp cold wind hit Tommy in the face, which surprised him on such a warm summers evening. Tommy buttoned up his coat and lit a John Player cigarette. He had stood on this spot many times and he had never before seen the strange mist that was currently hanging over the roof tops of the silent town below him.

Tommy was shocked to suddenly see a man walking up the hill towards him. "Where the hell did he come from?"

"The strangest bloke you ever did see," Sue recalls her Dad telling his guests. He wore a big black mutton coat and a black top hat, just like an out of date funeral director.

"Good morning to you, squire. May I trouble you for a light?"

Tommy struck a match and the man lit his small cheroot. "Thank you most kindly, sir. I bid you good day," and as the gentleman continued on his way, Tommy chuckled to himself. "Thank you most kindly, sir, I bid you good day!" certainly not the sort of language Tommy normally heard at work.

As Tommy embarked on his descent down the hill, he glanced back at the out of date funeral director and was dumbfounded to see that there was nobody there. Tommy stared in amazement at the empty stretch of road in front of him, where the funeral director should have been. The strange mist that was hanging in the air also started to evaporate in front of his eyes. Tommy turned and looked at the town below, just in time to see the mist hanging over the roof tops disappear, leaving the warm summer's morning that one would expect for that time of year.

Whiston Hospital

Sue also told me this little tale, which she personally witnessed for herself, along with a story my wife told me.

On the corner of the street where I live, a brand new hospital has just been completed. We could only watch as the old Victorian hospital, that had been the focal point of our little village for hundreds of years, was demolished bit by bit, to be replaced by a giant concrete carbuncle.

My wife, Elaine and my dad's partner, Sue are both nurses and they have both worked in the old hospital, and now both work in the new one. According to what they have both told me, on separate occasions, there could be ghosts in the new hospital, as well as the old one. Maybe they are confused with the new layout and don't know where to go. Here's what the girls told me.

Many years ago, Sue was working the night shift in the echoing Victorian wards of the old hospital. All of the patients were asleep and Sue and another nurse were sitting at the nurses' desk chatting. Suddenly, one of the patients started screaming and Sue and the other nurse rolled their eyeballs at each other. "Which one of the old dementia patients was having a nightmare?" they both thought. Except it wasn't a poor old dementia sufferer, it was Pat.

Pat was about 40 and was recovering from a minor

operation, certainly not the type of person to go screaming in the middle of the night. She was hysterical and she flung her arms around Sue and begged her to, "Get it off me!"

When Pat calmed down, she told Sue that she woke up because someone had hold of her ankles and was trying to pull her out of the bed. When she opened her eyes to see who it was, there was nobody there!"

The transition of moving patients and staff from the old hospital into the new one, was done in stages. My wife Elaine, who may I remind you says she doesn't believe in ghosts, was one of the first nurses to have her ward transferred to the new hospital. Elaine settled her patients and then took a look around the new ward. At the back of the ward was a door, which was locked. Elaine looked through the glass in the door and saw an almost empty room, just a few bags of building materials and a set of step ladders. Elaine asked her matron about the room and was told it would eventually be an extension of their ward. However, the room was not complete yet and therefore the door was to remain locked.

About ten-thirty that night, Elaine was settling her patients down for the night and looking forward to finishing her shift at eleven. Something caught her eye and she glanced up at the locked door. A man was staring straight at her through the glass in the door and he looked terrified. The man turned and ran out of view. Elaine had dealt with drug addicts roaming the wards before, looking for drugs to steal. She wasn't scared of them, her patients come first, and she ran to the door and looked through the glass but could only make out the building materials in the dim light.

She tried the door again but it was still locked.

Convinced there must be another entrance to the room, she buzzed security and within minutes a burly security guard was on the scene. Elaine and the guard knew each other well, having dealt with many incidents together over the years, so he knew she wouldn't call security for nothing. He told her there was another entrance to the room that should be locked and he would go and check it out. As Elaine waited on the ward, she saw the lights come on in the unfinished room and she looked through the glass. The security guard was standing in the room looking around and using his skeleton key, he opened the door that Elaine was looking through.

"There is no one here, Elaine," he told her, "and the other door was locked, so no one could have been in here."

Elaine told me, "Maybe I just imagined it."

But I wonder just who it is she is trying to kid.

To Nan

I was having a chat with my good friend and neighbour, Penny and I told her I was writing this book.

"Look at this," she said, and she opened a drawer and took out a small box of her most prized possessions. She took a piece of paper from the box. The paper had been folded into a small square and she carefully opened it out on the coffee table. The writing was fading and the whole thing was in danger of disintegrating altogether, only some crude yellowed cellotape holding it together. The handwriting was that of a child and I could still make out what it said.

Penny told me that her mother was only 50, when she died of pancreatic cancer, just like my mum. The day after her mum died, Penny was obviously exhausted and full of grief. Her friend told her to go to bed for a while and try to get some sleep. Her friend promised to stay over and baby sit for Penny's ten year old daughter, Kelly, so Penny went upstairs to rest.

Penny lay in bed trying to sleep. "Next minute," Penny told me," I could suddenly 'smell' my mum and then the bed depressed, as if someone had sat on the edge of the bed, next to me." Penny screamed and buried her head under the covers. Anything supernatural terrified the life out of Penny, even if it was her own mother. "Please, Mum, go away," Penny sobbed under the covers and she sobbed even more when her friend ran into the room and took Penny in her arms. Penny left that bedroom immediately and refused to ever enter it again.

The following morning, Penny sat little Kelly down at the kitchen table and gave her some cornflakes. She poured herself a strong coffee and lit yet another cigarette.

"Mummy, can I tell you something?" Little Kelly asked her Mum.

"Of course you can, darling," Penny replied, sitting herself down at the table next to Kelly. Penny stroked her little girl's hair and smiled at her. "Poor little thing must be missing her nan," Penny thought to herself.

"I was talking to my nan last night!"

Penny went stone cold. She stared into her daughters big brown expressive eyes. "Don't say things like that," Penny screamed at Kelly, "You know your nan is in Heaven."

Kelly fled up to her bedroom in tears, leaving Penny feeling terribly guilty, but try as she may, she could not bring herself to talk to Kelly.

"The following morning, I walked into the kitchen and put the kettle on," Penny continued to tell me. "I went to get the milk from the fridge and this letter was pinned to the fridge with a fridge magnet. I have kept it all these years."

I looked at the faded child-like handwriting once more. I have Penny's permission to tell you what it said.

To Nan.

If you can see this letter. My mum thinks I've gone off my rocker. She thinks I can't hear you, but I can. See you later.

Love, your Granddaughter. Kelly X

Mark Jones, Luke Jones and little Dixie

When my friend, Peter, was ten years old, he and his family moved into a new house. A brand new house, so new that most of the other houses on this new rural estate were not even finished yet. Peter went to explore his new neighbourhood and was delighted to find it was surrounded by fields of golden barley. He had moved to the countryside, nothing like the tough inner town area he had grown up in and to a ten year old boy this was paradise.

He was also delighted to find a ten feet high, sandstone wall that stretched for at least half a mile down a leafy lane. Looming over the top of the wall, Peter could see huge ancient trees and he knew that the 'haunted woods' had to be the next place to be explored. He found an abandoned old bike and propped it against the wall. Using the bike as a ladder, he was soon sitting on top of the wall. From here he could see that the woods were thick and densely overgrown. The woods looked like nobody had walked in them for years, just the sort of place to fire a ten year old's imagination.

Peter walked along the top of the wall until he found a suitable tree to climb down. The woods were so overgrown with intertwined tree branches leading down to the floor, that Peter had no problem reaching the ground. The thick undergrowth clung to his clothes and immediately 'sticky buds' began to embed themselves into

Peter's favourite red Liverpool Football Club woollen jumper. Peter cursed, as he knew from experience it would take him hours picking the sticky buds out of the wool. He took his jumper off and left it on the tree he had just climbed down.

Peter grabbed a big stick and continuing in just his t-shirt and jeans, he began to beat a path through the undergrowth. It wasn't long before he came across a pathway. It too was overgrown but it was easier to follow. A little further along, Peter caught a glimpse of a house through the trees. He froze and began to get a bit scared. Who would live in here? Could be a madman! Should he go back? Maybe go just a little bit further and take a peek.

Peter inched his way forward, with his heart thumping in his chest. The pathway led to a garden which was also wildly overgrown, nobody had tended to it for years. Peter crouched in the undergrowth and looked at the house. The house was impressive, with its two sandstone pillars holding up the sandstone canopy over the front steps. However, with some of the windows broken and boarded up, Peter wondered whether anyone still lived there. Just in case, he stuck to the outer edges of the garden and made his way around it.

Peter could see a big pond of water on the far side of the garden and it was almost totally covered in green slime. As Peter made his way towards the pond, his black plimsolled foot struck something hard and Peter fell face first into the undergrowth. He screamed in pain, as the thick thorn bushes scratched at his face and arms. If there is someone in that house, surely they have heard him now. Oh, sweet lord, don't let it be a madman. Peter climbed to his feet and crouched behind a tree but there did not seem to be any movement from the house. He looked down to see what he had fallen over and saw a small slab, standing upright in the ground. He used his stick to clear the undergrowth from the slab and bent down to take a look at it.

Here lies Mark Jones aged 11.

Next to this was another sandstone slab and again Peter scratched away at the undergrowth.

Here lies Luke Jones aged 9.

And next to this a smaller slab,

Here lies little Dixie.

"Hey!" a booming man's voice bellowed through the air and Peter turned to see a very angry looking old man standing at the front door of the house. The man had long white hair and a long scraggy white beard. His face was contorted with rage and he waved a walking stick menacingly in the air. Peter fled back into the woods in a state of terror. He ran through the undergrowth trying to find his way out when he spotted something red, his Liverpool jumper. Thank God he had left it on the tree and in one swift movement he grabbed his jumper and climbed the branch to the top of the wall. He dropped down on the other side and ran home as fast as his legs would carry him.

In the safety of his bedroom, Peter lay on his bed, getting

his breath back. He thought about the three makeshift headstones he had stumbled upon, two little boys and a dog. How had they died? Maybe the pond in the garden had something to do with it. Maybe the little dog had gotten into trouble in the pond and the boys had tried to save it, before getting into trouble themselves. Maybe the dog had tried to save them. Either way Peter decided he was not going back over that wall to face the madman.

So where is the ghost? I hear you say.

Well, many years later, Peter and his wife were on a night out in Liverpool town centre and at the end of the evening Peter and his wife climbed into a black hackney cab.

"Where to, mate?" the cabbie asked.

"Whiston, please."

"Ooh!" said the cabbie wearily, "Where about in Whiston?"

"Lickers Lane, do you know it?"

"Oh God! I knew you were going to say that," the cabbie groaned.

"Why? What's wrong, mate?" Peter asked, "Are you okay taking us there?"

"Yes, I will take you, mate, it's just that I am a bit apprehensive, that's all."

"Why's that?" Peter asked.

"I haven't had a fare to Lickers Lane for many years now

and I hoped I never would again. Has it still got that sandstone wall running the length of it?"

"Yes, it has," Peter told him.

"See, that's what scares me," the cabbie continued, "The last time I was on that lane was back in the 1970s and I ran into two ghosts. I dropped my fare off at the top end of the lane and turned the cab around. As I drove back down the lane with the wall on my left, two young boys ran into the road in front of me. The brakes on the cab screamed as I tried to avoid them, but it was too late. I was convinced I had run them both over, but to my amazement and utter horror the two boys ran straight through that sandstone wall as if it wasn't there. I have no idea who they were, but I'll tell you I wasn't hanging around to find out."

"I think I might know who they were," Peter told him, "Mark and Luke Jones."

"Who are they?" the cabbie asked.

"I don't know," Peter said, "But let me tell you a little tale that happened to me when I was ten."

A Highland Fling

"You are never going to find anywhere at such short notice," I told my wife Elaine, "It's the height of the summer season, everywhere is fully booked."

Still she persevered, trawling the internet trying to find us a small cottage in Scotland that we could rent for a week.

"I am sorry, the cottage is not available this week," was the response from every number she tried.

"How much can I go up to?" she asked me.

Normally fifty or sixty pounds a night is as much as we can afford, but as it was the height of the summer season and because I did not think she would find anywhere anyway, I agreed to a maximum of one hundred pounds a night.

I heard her speaking on the phone again, "Really, that sounds wonderful, can I just talk to my husband and call you back in a few minutes?"

"Six hundred for the week," she told me.

"Oh, Elaine, that's an awful lot of money."

"Just come and have a look at this, it should be one thousand two hundred pound a week. The agent has had a last minute cancellation and says we can have it from tomorrow for half price."

I looked at the computer screen and instantly realised why this place was so expensive, this was no cottage, it was a mansion. Three reception rooms, eight bedrooms, set slightly up the hill with immaculate lawns gently sloping down to the loch shore line. The house looked very old and had a Gothic spooky style to it, complete with the skeleton of a big stags head and antlers above the front door.

The house is owned by an extremely wealthy Kent land owner and this land owner is a personal friend of the Royal Family. Its isolated position makes it ideal for the Royals to escape the attentions of the press. I know that both Prince William and Prince Harry stay at the house, so out of respect for their privacy I am not going to name the house, or give any clues as to its location. The owner of the house would not normally rent it out at all, he doesn't exactly need the money, however a local letting agent managed to convince him that security would be better if the house was occupied and not left empty for long periods of time.

As we drove up the driveway, the house took my breath away as it came into view. Seeing it on a computer screen is one thing, but when you see it in real life, it was fantastic. I went around to the back of the house and located the key safe. As instructed I entered the last four digits of my home phone number and the key safe popped open to reveal a large old fashioned key.

We opened the back door and stepped inside. It was like stepping back in time, two maybe even three hundred years and I loved it. Elaine however, who may I remind you does not believe in ghosts, was not so sure.

"Oh, Carle, I'm not sure I like this."

"Well you better get used to it because we have spent a lot of money and travelled a long way for this, so we are staying."

A small tin box sat on the otherwise empty kitchen table and I opened it to reveal a whole load of keys, each one carefully labelled. I took the key labelled 'front door' and opened the big old oak front door. The view of the loch and the surrounding forest was magnificent and I breathed in the fresh air with a huge smile on my face. This was proper lord and lady of the manor stuff.

All over the house, especially lining the walls of the wide impressive staircase, there were old-fashioned hand painted portraits of old people in Victorian clothing. The sort of portraits you would associate with the eyes moving and watching your every move. Elaine swears she saw the eyes of some of the portraits moving, but I managed to convince her that it was just the way the artist had painted them, to give the impression that the eyes were moving. I don't know who I was trying to convince, Elaine or myself.

As I explored the bedrooms, I wondered which bed the future King of England had slept in. I guessed it was probably a double bed in the largest room and of course, that's the one we chose. I loaded the open fire with some small bits of fire wood and firelighters and soon had a roaring fire going in the big old fire place. Two large and well deserved Bacardi and Cokes were poured and we settled down in front of the TV and the fire, with a selection of crisps, nuts and other nibbles.

Due to the copious amount of alcohol consumed, I slept like a lamb on that first night. Elaine claims she never slept a wink. As soon as the dawn started to flood the bedroom, Elaine was shaking me awake. She climbed out of bed and peeped out onto the landing.

"What are you doing?"

"Will you come to the bathroom with me; I'm dying for a wee."

"Are you nuts? Look at the time, go for a wee yourself! What's got into you anyway?"

"Please, Carle, I'm scared, I heard someone on the landing in the middle of the night."

"Oh, don't be silly, go on, go and have a wee. I will guard the landing for you and then I am going to take Dixie out for a walk."

The weather was beautiful that first day and we walked our big Golden Retriever, Dixie along the banks of the loch. That night, we once again curled up in front of the fire with a large Bacardi and in the early hours of the morning I was awoken from a sound sleep by Elaine screaming, as she ran into the bedroom and dived into bed with me.

"What's wrong?"

"I think I just saw someone on the landing."

"You think?"

"Well, I can't find the light switch for the landing, so it was like a shadow."

"Oh, it's nothing, go back to sleep," I yawned.

"I swear, Carle, I saw him, it was an old man."

The following day, I drove into the nearest town for some more supplies, which took about an hour. When I got back Elaine came running out of the house and threw her arms around my neck.

"Hey, what's the matter?"

"Oh, Carle, why were you so long? I have been terrified to move away from the fire. We are not alone in there, Carle."

"Oh, come on, I am back now, let's go through to the kitchen and get this food on the go, you feel okay in the kitchen don't you?"

"Yes, it's just these stairs and the landing," she said, as we stood at the open front door, looking up the magnificent flight of stairs.

Elaine settled down over the next couple of days, she did, however, make sure that the dog and I were never out of her sight. If I drove into town to buy more supplies, Elaine would always insist on her and Dixie coming with me, which is something she would never have done before, or since.

On the fifth day, the weather was fantastic once again and Elaine and I were sat in one of the huge bay windows at the front of the house. We had the big old sash windows wide open and a gentle breeze was cooling us down. The loch looked stunning, like a mirror and the whole moment could not have been more peaceful and perfect. I asked Elaine if she fancied having a little 'play' in the bedroom and she smiled and said, "Okay, I will just go and have a bath."

As she disappeared up the stairs, I immersed myself in a small paperback that I had found in the house. It was written over a hundred years ago, by the teacher of the time at the local school. She had taken it upon herself to research the local history of the tiny hamlet that she served, and I was so engrossed in the tales and legends of the local area that I totally forgot about Elaine.

After what must have been more than an hour, I remembered Elaine was in the bath, but I was not overly concerned knowing what women are like in the bath. I carried on reading my book, occasionally glancing up at the magnificent scenery around me thinking, "Wow, all this happened right here."

I glanced at my watch; it must be two hours since Elaine went for a bath. How long does it take for a woman to have a bath?" I walked into the hallway and Dixie was lying at the base of the stairs, looking at me with those big soulful eyes of his. I stepped over him and climbed the stairs, shouting to Elaine as I reached the landing. There were two bathrooms and I did not know which one she was in. I tried the door of the first bathroom and it was locked!

I know from more than thirty years of living with this girl, that she always closes the bathroom door, but she would never lock herself in when there is only the two of us in the house, especially this house! I knocked on the bathroom door.

"Elaine?"

"Carle, is that you?"

"Of course it's me, you daft cow, who else would it be?"

I heard the water splashing in the bath and the small lock being slid back on the bathroom door. I pushed the door open and Elaine was stood there, shivering and wrapping a towel around herself.

"Why didn't you come for me?" she cried, "I called for you and Dixie and neither of you came."

"I'm sorry, Babe, I didn't hear you, what's wrong? Are you okay?"

"Did you come in here about an hour ago?" she asked me.

"No. Why?"

"Well someone did! The door opened by itself."

"It will be the breeze blowing in from downstairs," I promised.

"Try moving the bathroom door!" she demanded.

I pushed the bathroom door and for the first time since we had been there, I noticed that the bathroom carpet was a very luxurious thick shag pile and the door needed a good strong push to move it. There was no way any breeze, or even a strong wind blowing through the house could have moved that door.

Enough was enough for Elaine, who wanted to go home immediately. I somehow managed to convince her to stay, even though I could not explain how that door could open by itself, whilst she was in the bath. I tried to convince her that it could have been Dixie, but Elaine pointed out that although she never locked the bathroom door, it had an old fashioned 'latch' which she did put on.

"And in any case watch this," she said as she walked across the landing to the top of the stairs, "Dixie, come here boy."

Dixie was lying at the bottom of the stairs and immediately sat up when Elaine called his name. Dixie adored Elaine and would not normally leave her side, but he would not come up the stairs.

"Have you not noticed?" she asked me, "in nearly a week we have been here, Dixie has not been up the stairs once."

On our final full day, I told Elaine I would need to drive into town for some more logs and once again she insisted that she and the dog were coming with me. As we drove along the dirt track that bordered the loch, we passed a lovely little cottage with a typical little white picket fence and a white picket gate. An old man, with snow white hair and a bushy white beard, was standing in front of the white picket fence. He was dressed in full traditional tartan complete with kilt and sporran and he smiled and waved at me as I drove past. I laughed and waved back, I wondered whether he dressed like that every day, or whether he was just entertaining the tourists.

"What are you laughing at?" Elaine asked me.

"That old man waving at us," I said.

"What old man?"

Elaine was sitting in the passenger seat next to me and, being the nervous passenger that she is, she always watches where we are going. I pulled the car into the next passing point.

"Did you not just see that old man in the kilt?

"No," she said.

I quickly spun the car around and drove back a couple of hundred yards, but you guessed it. The cottage with the little picket fence was there, but there was no sign of the old man dressed in tartan.

The next morning, a very relieved Elaine was happy to be going home. I asked her if she would ever stay there again and she said, "Never!"

"Not even if it was half price again?" I asked

"Not even if it was free!" she confidently announced.

Amazing coincidences

When I did my psychology degree at university, one of the Parapsychology lectures I attended was based on amazing coincidences. One of the stories I remember from that lecture, was of a man whose job it was to clean telephone boxes. One day, he was cleaning the windows of an old red phone box, when the phone began to ring. Out of curiosity, he picked up the receiver and said, "Hello?" On the other end of the line was his best friend calling him with some important information.

"John," the cleaner asked his friend, "What number have you rang?"

"Your house, of course," his friend replied.

"I am not at home; I am in a phone box."

****

Here are a few amazing coincidences that have happened to me personally. I am sure you can recall similar things happening to you. Let me know about them and maybe your story will be in my next book.

Jean O'Hare

By far the worst thing that has ever happened to me was the death of my beautiful mum, Jean. I was twenty-one and loving life, when that terrible disease, cancer, took her away from us. She was just forty-five years old.

When my mum and dad first met as teenagers, my dad had a best friend called George. George met a girl called Mary and much to my dad and George's delight, my mum and Mary became best friends. The four teenagers were inseparable and George stood as best man when my dad married my mum, with Mary by her side as bridesmaid. A few weeks later my mum and dad repaid the compliment at George and Mary's wedding.

Both couples went on to have three children, two girls and a boy and the families lived across the road from each other in the same street. When my mum was diagnosed with cancer, Mary was devastated, as we all were. Imagine our horror when just a few months after my mum died, Mary too was diagnosed with cancer. Mary fought hard to beat the disease, but sadly lost that fight in the end.

When I heard that 'Aunty Mary' had passed away, I went round to see 'Uncle George'.

"I am so sorry, mate."

"I know you are, son," he replied, "You know what we are going through."

As he made us both a cup of, tea he said, "Hey, Carle, you won't believe this, how about this for an amazing coincidence. Towards the end, Mary knew she only had a few days to live and she did not want to die in the house. We had all lived so happily in this house and she wanted me and the kids to continue to feel happy here. So when she was ready, she asked me to call for the ambulance to take her to the Marie Curie hospice, where she would see out her final days."

As George pushed Mary's wheelchair into the hospice, a young nurse with short blond hair came walking towards them.

"Hello, Mary, are you okay, love? I will be looking after you while you're staying with us," the young nurse smiled.

"Well! Will you look at that, George," Mary said turning to her husband, "I told you I was going to be alright, look who has come to take care of me."

Mary pointed at the nurse's name badge.

"You won't believe this, Carle," Uncle George continued, "The nurse's name was Jean O'Hare!"

George then proudly showed me the watch he was wearing and explained that it was given to him by Nurse Jean, to make sure he didn't stay in the pub too long and miss visiting time at the hospice.

"There was only one thing different about Nurse Jean and your mum though," George continued, "The nurse was from the Dingle area of town, not the Huyton area that we are from."

A cold shiver ran through me.

"George my mum is from the Dingle, that is where she grew up. She was very proud of her Dingle roots, her mum and most of her family still live there."

"Oh, my God, of course she was," George said with a sudden sense of realisation, "I had totally forgotten that!"

Jimmy's Page

One beautiful summer's day, my family and I were in the garden enjoying the sunshine. There was me and my wife Elaine, Elaine's sister Lynn, Lynn's husband George and three kids. Someone suggested we should go somewhere on such a lovely day and George suggested a ghost hunt.

"You must know some places to take us, Carle," he said.

"Yeah, let's go on a ghost hunt," the kids cried.

"Okay, what about the sunken graveyard behind the Cathedral in town, I have read many stories about that place and we could visit the Cathedral as well?"

Soon we were walking down the sloping pathway that leads to the sunken graveyard behind Liverpool's Anglican Cathedral. A shiver of anticipation ran down my spine. I had read many stories about this place, but this was the first time I had visited. Although it is officially a graveyard, it is actually a beautiful green open space and the kids soon dispersed in different directions. As we walked around, I pointed out sights of ghostly interest, including the beautifully carved name Little Grace.

Legend has it Little Grace was born to a servant girl and her master. When the little girl died, who knows how, the unscrupulous master had the child thrown into a tomb in the sandstone face of the graveyard. Many people have reported seeing a child's hand coming out of the sandstone and some claim to have seen and spoken to Little Grace, including the stonemason, who so expertly carved her name into the sandstone, in a bid to give her a marked grave of her own.

After leaving the graveyard, we went into the Cathedral and explored the amazing interior. There are plenty of glass display cabinets, containing all manner of things and as I stared at the large open book in one of the cabinets, I read the little brass plate that explained what the book was about. It was a book of remembrance and it contained all the names of Liverpool soldiers who had died in conflict, including conflicts such as Northern Ireland and the Falkland Islands.

The little brass plate also informed me that the pages of the book are turned regularly, to save any one page from discolouring and to make sure each soldiers name has a chance to be displayed. I looked at the list of names and immediately realised there was a whole bunch called 'Jones', my wife's surname. One name in the middle of the list of 'Joneses' fixed my attention.

242693254 Kingsman J.J Jones.

Died in action on 18th of July 1972.

I recognised the date immediately, it was Elaine's brother. I called Elaine and her sister Lynn over and showed them what I had found.

"Just a coincidence," I can hear the cynics shouting.

Maybe. It is, however, quite remarkable that the book

happened to be open on that page, when Jimmy's two baby sisters were there to see it.

The Birds

If birds could speak to us, I wonder what they would say? Probably tell us to stop killing each other, or more importantly stop killing them.

I once watched an amazing documentary on the TV. A large male parrot was quite happy to show its handler and the film crew what it could do, in exchange for peanuts. A tray was placed in front of the parrot and on the tray were about 15 different shapes. Some triangles, some circles, some squares, etc. The shapes were made of different materials, some wood, some plastic, some metal. The shapes were also different colours.

"What would you like to ask Jack?" the handler asked the film crew. "Let me give you an example," she said and then, addressing the parrot, she said, "Jack, what material is the blue triangle made from?" The parrot scanned the tray for a couple of seconds and then looked at the handler and clearly said, "Wood."

"Very good, Jack," the handler said, as she rewarded the parrot with a peanut. The film crew were invited to ask Jack their own questions and every single time, the parrot gave the correct answer. "Which proves," the handler announced, "that birds are capable of lateral thinking. Jack was not just memorising the shape and colour of a wooden block, he was actually listening to the question and studying his options, before giving his answer."

They say that ravens guard the Tower of London. Is that because they just happen to live there? Or have people actually sat and observed their behaviour over the years? And did they come to the conclusion that they do actually appear to be guarding something?

Here are a couple of stories about birds. One that happened to me a couple of years ago and one that happened to my wife Elaine only this morning, (summer 2014), which inspired me to write about the birds.

A year or two ago, I was sitting in my taxi, reading ghost stories. The story was about a certain patch of land at the junction of two roads in Liverpool. The patch of land was said to contain a 'Fairy Circle' and legend had it, the circle was guarded by a large black crow. The author of the story recommended that anyone thinking of exploring the circle for themselves, should not go alone, don't go after dark, don't enter the circle itself and lastly, be very wary of the big black crow.

I half laughed to myself and made a mental note to visit the fairy circle the next time I took a customer to that area of town. Sure enough, later that day, I picked up a passenger who wanted to be taken in the general direction of the fairy circle, so I couldn't wait to drop him off and go in search of this little piece of alleged paranormal activity.

After dropping my passenger off, I quickly scanned the ghost story again, to determine exactly where this fairy circle was located and then I opened my A to Z of Liverpool streets and went in search of my goal. As I drove up and down the same stretch of road several times,

I noticed how all of the side streets had names connected with the ancient Druids. One street was even called, Druids Lane.

I also noticed that daylight was fast diminishing and I recalled the author's warning 'not to visit the fairy circle after dark'. Again, I half laughed to myself and pulled the car over to the kerb to check my A to Z again. I lit a cigarette and scanned the page of the A to Z, and then I looked out of the open window and flicked my cigarette ash, as I tried to determine exactly where I was.

It was only then that I saw it. A huge black crow was sitting silently on the grass verge, looking at me. As soon as we made eye contact with each other, the crow spread its huge wings and screamed at me. I am sure most people know what a squawking crow sounds like and this big beast was up there with the best of them.

I am sorry to tell you folks, but it terrified the life out of me and I hit the accelerator and got the hell out of there. Some ghost hunter I am, eh? I haven't tried to find the fairy circle since!

So what happened only this morning?

I have mentioned in my other stories, that my wife, Elaine, is the biggest sceptic in the world, however, she does claim to have what she calls 'women's intuition'. Elaine is a nurse in the hospital and if she is on the early shift, I sleep on the settee, as she says my snoring keeps her awake. At 6am this morning, I stirred from my slumber on the settee, as I heard Elaine coming down the stairs. She then opened the front door and I heard her gasp.

"Hey! Stop that," she shouted, "Go on! Shoo!"

"What are you doing?" I grumbled.

"It's okay, it's only a cat. Why don't you go and get in bed?"

When she came home from work that afternoon, she told me what happened. The alarm clock had just woken her up and she hit the snooze button and was happily grabbing those last few minutes of bliss before you have to get up. Suddenly a loud urgent tapping sound on the window roused her from her slumber. A magpie was sitting on the ledge outside the window, looking straight at her and frantically pecking at the glass.

Elaine closed her eyes and tried to ignore the magpie, determined to grab those last few precious minutes of sleep. Then the pecking at the glass stopped, only to be replaced by a scratching sound. Elaine opened her eyes and was amazed to see the magpie standing on one leg, scratching the window with its other claw. The magpie realised that Elaine was looking once more and franticly pecked at the window again.

Elaine loves her animals and her 'women's intuition' told her something was wrong. She was not afraid of the old wives' tale, that a single magpie represented sorrow or bad luck. She was more concerned that the magpie was asking for help. As soon as she climbed out of bed the magpie flew away. She looked out of the window, but could see nothing amiss in the back garden.

That's when she came down stairs and opened the front

door, only to be confronted by an injured magpie laying in our front garden, with a cat trying to finish what it had started. Two other magpies were frantically squawking at the cat and flapping their wings trying to scare it away. The cat scarpered when Elaine came on the scene and the other magpies calmed down and went to the aid of their injured friend. Elaine knew from the experiences of our own sadly departed cats, that the magpie may just be shocked or stunned and sure enough after a few minutes it flew away with its friends.

So, was the frantic magpie at our bedroom window actively seeking Elaine's help? I think so.

Ghostly goings on, on the motorway

My brother in law is a lorry driver. I have known George for more than 30 years now and as we are both married to a pair of very close sisters, George and I are good friends too. I remember many years ago when he passed his HGV licence and his Wife Lynn bought him a Yorkie Bar. George had always been a driver anyway, delivering or picking up goods in a van, since he passed his driving test first time, aged 17.

He told me in all his years travelling up and down the motorway network, he has only ever witnessed two incidents that he cannot explain. Maybe the first little occurrence can be explained away, but certainly not the second one and I have known George for long enough to know that he does not make up stupid stories.

The first occasion was when George was very young and was driving a van to Hampshire, with a friend. I asked him why they were going there and he laughed and wouldn't tell me, so I guess the two teenagers were up to no good. Anyway, the two boys had made an early start and as they travelled south down the M6 motorway towards Stoke, the early morning mist was rolling across the motorway from the adjacent fields.

George kept to a steady 60mph because of the mist and his friend had his head buried in the map, as he tried to work out their route.

"Wow! Where did he come from?" George suddenly shouted and his friend looked up just in time to catch a glimpse of the man standing on the hard shoulder, as they drove past him.

George told me the man they saw was old compared to them, with a bald head and spectacles. He wore a smart suit with a shirt and tie, with a brown trench coat over his suit. He looked like a typical office worker, although a little outdated and he held out a hand, as if gesturing for help. The man was looking directly at George and watched him drive past, but there was no way George was going to risk stopping in such misty conditions. And in any case George did not like what he had just witnessed one little bit.

"He just appeared from nowhere, in front of my eyes," George told me.

"It is possible," I tried to reason, "That this bloke's car has skidded off the motorway and he has walked out of the mist and onto the hard shoulder in an attempt to get help?"

"Maybe," George conceded, "But that's not what I saw. There was little if any mist around him, he just seemed to step out of nowhere. From a place I couldn't see, into a place I could."

George is convinced that the stretch of the M6 where he saw the 'office worker ghost' is cursed. As a lorry driver, he keeps tuned in to the local radio stations, listening for any travel news of accidents or other hold-ups on the network.

"Whenever there is a report of a crash on the motorway, nine times out of ten, it will be on that stretch of the motorway," George continued, "and I can't understand why, because it is a nice straight, flat stretch of road, I am convinced that stretch of motorway must have been built over an old burial site of some sort."

What George saw on that same stretch of motorway early one morning, only goes towards strengthening his belief, and it may account for some of the unexplained accidents that have occurred on that stretch of road.

The sun had just come up and George was pleased that he had made an early start to beat the traffic. The motorway was virtually empty, apart from one or two other lorry drivers who had the same idea as George and had made an early start. George's 40 ton articulated truck was making good progress down the inside lane at 60mph, the maximum speed his lorry was governed to. George was slowly gaining on another lorry in front of him, so he indicated to overtake and checked his mirror.

George needed to ease off the accelerator and tease his brakes because another artic was coming up the middle lane from behind him. The artic still had its headlights full on, even though it was now daylight and it obviously was not governed to 60mph like George's was, because it was gaining on George at a colossal speed.

Despite it being a bright sunny start to the day, there was a strong gusty wind blowing across the motorway and George thought the driver of the approaching lorry must be a complete idiot. As the lorry thundered past him, George gave the driver a one fingered salute, then he froze with fear as he watched the wheels on the rear left-hand side of the artic's trailer rise up from the road. In all his years of driving some of the biggest vehicles on the road, George had never seen the wheels of a 40 ton artic leave the road like that, and he was convinced that a catastrophe was about to occur.

George called upon all of his driving experience and training and started to brake his lorry but without braking hard, praying there was nothing coming from behind him at speed. The lorry driver on the inside lane in front of him was breaking hard and George had no choice, other than to swing his lorry into the middle lane.

That's when George could not believe his eyes. The 40 ton artic truck that was about to topple over in front of him, had completely disappeared!

As George passed the lorry on the inside lane, he looked across at the driver. The driver looked back at George with a look of wide eyed terror and shrugged his shoulders. George tried to indicate to the driver to pull into the next service station, but despite George waiting for 20 minutes in the next services, the other driver never showed, leaving George with no choice other than to continue with his delivery and still ponder to this day, how a 40 ton articulated lorry can simply vanish off the face of the earth.

Fullwood Park

It is a sad fact of life, that the older you get, the more funerals you start going to. Just a few short weeks after cremating my Uncle Keith, I found myself back in exactly the same crematorium, mourning the loss of my Uncle Jimmy. After the service, we all went back to the pub where my aunties and cousins had put on a fine spread of food. I went outside for a cigarette and got talking to my cousin, Joe, who I hadn't seen for a while.

"How are you, mate?" he smiled, "Are you still on the taxis?"

"Yes, mate, I am, as well as writing a book."

"Really? What is it about?"

"It's a collection of short ghost stories," I told him.

"Wow, do you want to hear a ghost story?"

"Yes, go on."

"I have never believed in ghosts," he continued, "but something happened to me and my mate only last year, right in there, as it happens," and he pointed down the road.

About fifty yards away, there were two magnificent square sandstone pillars, each easily 12 feet in height. Each pillar had been elaborately carved by some master craftsman a

145

long time ago and on one pillar the words 'Fullwood Park' had been carved, whilst the other read 'Private Road'.

"Have you ever been in there?" Joe asked me.

"No I haven't."

"There are some massive big old houses in there, mate, some of them hundreds of years old."

Joe continued to tell me that he was working as a joiner for a local builder. His boss sent him and his young apprentice to price up a job in one of the big old houses in Fullwood Park. The house was now split into six luxury apartments and his boss gave him the keys to apartment number six, on the top floor. The owner was out at work and Joe was instructed to let himself in and measure up for a new kitchen. It didn't take long and as they left the apartment, Joe was careful to lock the door with the deadlock key.

As Joe and his apprentice reached the hallway at the bottom of the stairs, the big old oak front door of the building, which had been wide open when they arrived, so they saw no reason to close it, suddenly slammed shut with tremendous force. Joe and his apprentice were frozen to the spot and looked at each other, neither of them knowing what to say. Joe marched across the hallway and grabbed the big wooden handle of the front door, but it refused to budge.

"Here, let me have a go," his mate said, but despite the attempts of two joiners and one chisel that Joe happened to have in his belt, the door would not move.

"I don't like this, Joe, how can a big heavy door slam shut on its own like that?"

"I don't know," Joe confessed.

The two men suddenly felt the floor beneath their feet start to vibrate and this quickly escalated into a tremble. The big old front door started to shake violently in its frame and the two men fled up the stairs, not knowing what they were running from, or whether running up the stairs was a good idea. Joe and his apprentice frantically banged on the doors of the separate apartments as they ran up the stairs, begging for someone to let them in. Amazingly, not a single person seemed to be at home and Joe and his mate reached the top floor and used the keys to get into apartment six, slamming the door shut behind them. The whole building shook for a few more seconds, then quickly slowed down and stopped.

Joe's young apprentice was looking at him, with a look of sheer terror on his face. "What the hell, Joe?"

"I don't know, let me think." Joe's heart was pounding in his chest and his mind was working overtime. How to get out when you are stuck on the top floor and the only way out is through the front door. They needed help, who could he call? His boss? No, not a very nice man, he would be furious.

Tony! Yes! Tony, a fellow joiner, was working on another job, less than a mile away. Joe brought Tony's number up on his mobile and was mightily relieved when after only two rings, Tony's voice said, "What's up?"

"Where are you?" Joe gasped.

"You know where I am, on that job in Lark Lane."

"Get round to Fullwood Park as fast as you can, number 16."

"Why?"

"Just hurry up will you, we need your help here."

"Okay. I'm on my way."

A few minutes later, Joe watched from the apartment's front window as Tony's car screeched to a halt outside. Tony leapt from his car and frantically pushed at the front door, but the door wouldn't budge. Joe shouted down for him to wait, they were coming down. Joe and his apprentice virtually ran down the stairs and Joe grabbed and twisted the round wooden door knob, but still the front door refused to open. Joe opened the letter box to talk to Tony.

"Here, Tony, take the keys and see if you can open the door from the outside."

Tony took the keys and could see immediately that the door had a Yale lock and a deadlock. He put the Yale key in the lock and although it turned, the door still wouldn't open. He put the big Mortice key into the deadlock and heard it click open, as he turned the key. He opened the front door, to be confronted by two very relieved, ashen-faced men.

"The dead lock was on, how did you manage to lock

yourselves in?"

Joe was quick to thank Tony and made some half-hearted excuse about the door. Tony drove away looking confused and not entirely convinced.

"Listen," Joe told his apprentice, "we can't tell anyone at work about this, they will think we are nuts."

"I agree, but what if the boss wins the contract and we get sent back to do the job?"

"We'll cross that bridge when we come to it."

"I am not going back in there, not for a million pounds."

"No, neither am I. Come on, let's get out of here."

Luckily, Joe managed to convince his boss that the job would be a nightmare, as it was on the top floor and not worth the hassle. They did, after all, have more lucrative projects in the pipeline and reluctantly his boss agreed to let one of his competitors take the work, much to Joe's relief.

John will be fine

The following little tale was told to me by a delightful nurse, called Jane. I had the pleasure of driving Jane from one hospital to another and back again, and the story she told me concerns her mother, Doris.

72 years old, Doris couldn't sleep. It was the middle of the night and yet her bedroom was stiflingly hot, due to the beautiful summer weather. She was also terribly worried about her son, John, who was due to undergo open heart surgery as soon as the hospital called him. Doris knew everything there was to know about open heart surgery. Her own father was one of the very first people to undergo the procedure and he lived to a ripe old age. She had always read anything new on the subject, ever since.

She threw the thin bed cover onto the floor and lay on the bed with no covers on, but still she felt like she couldn't breathe. She longed to open the bedroom window and let some fresh air in, but she had a phobia about burglars and open windows at night, as she lived on her own.

Her underwear and her nightdress felt damp against her sweating skin, so she sat on the edge of the bed and did something she would never normally dream of. She lifted her nightdress over her head, unclipped her bra and slipped out of her panties. She lay back down and felt a little bit more comfortable now she was out of her sticky clothes, even though she felt slightly uncomfortable being naked.

A little while later, still unable to sleep, Doris decided to go for a 'wee'. She sat on the edge of the bed and picked her nightdress up off the floor. It was force of habit that she should dress to go to the bathroom, but on this occasion she just couldn't be bothered and scurried to the bathroom with her hands covering her bits. As she came back out of the bathroom, she switched the bathroom light off. She never bothered to switch the landing light on, because there was enough light shining in from her bedside lamp in the bedroom.

As she walked across the landing, towards her bedroom, she saw something move in the shadows at the top of the stairs. She froze with fear and squinted into the semi-darkness. Did she just see something then, or was it her imagination? She backed slowly into her bedroom, not daring to take her eyes from the top of the stairs. She felt the back of her legs hit the bed and automatically sat down. She stared through the open bedroom door at the shadows on top of the staircase.

There was definitely a man standing there, trying to hide in the shadows of the wall. Doris could not make out any of his facial features, but she could see the left side of his head and his left arm. She knew instantly that it was a ghost, because there was enough light for her to have seen a real person.

"This man was like a negative of a photograph," was how she described it later. Doris was so petrified she thought she was about to die. And worse still, she was naked! Naked in front of a man! Oh, the shame of it!

"Please, get out of my house," she whispered.

The 'Negative Man' quickly turned and headed down the stairs.

"I even heard his footsteps going down the stairs," Doris later told her two daughters.

Jane and her sister Lindsey took turns of staying with their Mum after that night, because poor old Doris was terrified out of her wits.

"What did it want?" "Will it come back?"

Jane's sister, Lindsey, had a friend who recommended a local spiritual church. Jane and her sister sat at the table with their mum, drinking tea and asked her what she thought. But Doris was not too keen on the idea; she had never been much of a churchgoer.

"We will all go together," Jane promised, "Maybe we might be able to speak to someone who can put your mind at rest."

Lindsey was staring at the mantelpiece above the fire. On the mantelpiece there was a framed photograph of her granddad, Doris's Dad. The photograph had been there ever since Lindsey could remember, but now she saw something different about it and she stood up to take a closer look. She picked up the frame and took it back to the table with her.

"What are you doing with that?" Doris asked.

Jane ran her finger across the photo to make sure there

was no marks or smudges on the glass.

"Look at this!" she told her mum and her sister.

Jane told me that her granddad was wearing a smart blazer in the photograph and on his blazer, right where his heart would be, was a bright blue spot.

"It was a colour so nice, I don't think I have ever seen that colour before, or since and it is hard to describe," Jane told me. Doris admitted that she had never noticed the blue spot before either and Lindsey stood up and took a butter knife from the drawer.

"What are you doing?" Doris asked nervously.

"I am just going to unclip the back of the frame and take the photograph out while we have a look at it."

"Oh, leave it, please," Doris begged, "that photo has been in that frame for years."

"It is only little clips, Mum; I will put it back in a minute."

As Lindsey turned the photograph face up on the table, Jane gasped and looked at her sister.

"What's wrong?" Doris asked.

"The blue spot we have just seen on the photo, Mum, look! It's gone!"

Doris was demented by now and started to cry.

"I think we should give this spiritual church a go, Mum. What do you think?"

"Okay." Doris agreed, "It's got to be worth a try, I can't go on like this."

The three women walked into the spiritualist church at 7pm on Thursday night, as that is when they were told the weekly meetings would take place. However, the place was empty, apart from one woman putting tea cups out on a table.

"Hello," the woman smiled, "Can I help you?"

"I am sorry," Jane said, "We were told that there would be a spiritualist meeting here at seven."

"Normally it is, girls," the woman smiled. She looked maybe about sixty, but she looked good and looked a lot younger.

"We have had to put it back a bit this week and we are starting at 7.30, but you are more than welcome. Come and take a seat. Would you like some tea?"

Doris and her daughters sat down at the table and the woman brought over a tray of tea and biscuits.

"Well, my name's Pat," she smiled, as she poured the tea, waiting for a response from any of the three women that were staring at her.

"Oh, yes, sorry. I'm Jane, this is my sister, Lindsey and this is our mum, Doris. She thinks she saw a ghost at the top of the stairs."

As soon as the words came out of her mouth, Jane felt terrible. Why did she have to go and blurt it out like that?

It sounded really insensitive.

"Your mum did see a ghost," Pat said, "and he is really sorry about that. He is standing behind your mum, right now."

Doris threw her hand to her mouth and a frightened, "Ooh" came out.

"Don't be scared, Doris," Pat said, as she leaned across the table and placed her hand on Doris's hand, "He says he is your dad."

"My dad?" Doris gasped. Jane and Lindsay just sat there staring at Pat with their mouths wide open like Venus Flytraps.

"He is really sorry that you saw him standing at the top of the stairs like that, he knows that he has really scared you. But he wants you to know that he is always looking out for you and he would never let anything hurt you. It's just that he has been so worried about you lately, and he wants me to give you a message."

"What is it?" Doris gasped.

"He says, 'John is going to be fine, just like I was'."

"Does that mean anything to you?"

Kenny meets death

Coming towards the end of writing this book, I decided to print off a hard copy and sort it into some kind of contents. I am not the best when it comes to computers and I just about know how to use Microsoft Word for typing and general internet and Hotmail. I put a brand new original HP ink into my old printer, but still could not get it to print. I needed help.

My lifelong friend, Kenny, was a cutting-edge scientist before ill health forced him into early retirement. Being pretty much confined to his desk at home every day, Kenny focused all his energy into his second biggest love in life, computers. I am convinced that Kenny could take a computer apart, screw by tiny screw and make it work better when he had put it back together again. I hadn't spoken to him in ages and as I drove past his flat on one of my taxi journeys, I pulled the car over.

"Hello, mate," I said, as he answered his phone.

"Hello, stranger, let me guess! You are stuck on your computer?"

"Oh, I am sorry, mate. Am I that predictable? I am sorry it's been a while."

"Don't you worry, mate, I know how hard you work." This was true, Kenny had in the past worked as the controller in our taxi office and bloody good at it he was too, as you would expect from Kenny.

"What are you stuck with?" he asked.

"My printer won't work and I would not normally bother you, but Elaine has also bought a new 'Smart TV' and she doesn't know how to use it, she keeps saying, 'Get Kenny round.'"

"So, you want me to come round to your house and sort your missus out again?"

"Ha ha. Yes, please." He always did have a way with words.

"Where are you?" he asked.

"Outside your flat."

"I knew you were going to say that, you cheeky little git," he laughed. "Give me five minutes".

There was no need for handshakes as he climbed into my car, just big smiles from the both of us.

"How are you, mate?" I asked.

"Okay now," he said.

"What do you mean?"

He lifted up his shirt to reveal a fat scar, running vertically down the length of his torso.

"Ouch, what happened there?"

"Open heart surgery."

Kenny told me that the surgeon who had operated on him was amazed at Kenny's rapid recovery. Kenny had in fact been dead for 8 hours and 47 minutes, while the surgeon literally took Kenny's heart out of his body and repaired it on a 'work bench'. Just like some mechanic in a diesel garage! Kenny's body and mind were kept alive by machines.

Another thing that astounded the surgeon, something he checked several times, by subjecting Kenny to a series of x-rays was that although Kenny admitted to being a very heavy smoker, his lungs were totally clean and clear.

"When can I go home?" Kenny asked his surgeon.

"Normally a patient would spend several weeks in recovery after the procedure you have had, Kenny, but you seem remarkably well after just a few days."

"So, can I go home?"

"Yes. I think you can, if you promise to take things easy. Just one thing still puzzles me, how can your lungs be so clear after all the smoking you have done?"

Kenny just smiled, "You're the doctor. You tell me".

"I don't know," the doctor confessed.

"I have never owned a car in my life," Kenny told him. "Anywhere I have ever needed to go to, I have walked there and back. Maybe this cardiovascular theory is true. Every day of my life, I have walked and breathed in fresh air."

It was great having Kenny round at our house again, and he quickly showed me what I was doing wrong with my printer. He then sat drinking coffee with Elaine, as he showed her the features of her new TV. When I was driving him back home, I told him the reason I needed the printer was because I was writing a book of ghost stories.

"Really? Let me have a look, I will edit them if you want me to."

"Have you ever seen a ghost Kenny?"

"No, I can tell you something that happened to me when I was a kid though."

I pulled the car into the lay-by outside his flat and switched the engine off.

"When I was about ten, I had too many teeth and seven of them needed to be taken out, in order for the others to grow into their natural position."

Kenny's mum was worried that taking seven teeth out at once would be too traumatic for him and the dentist agreed. He assured Kenny's mum that only one tooth a week would be extracted. Older readers will remember that the dentist previously used gas to knock his patients unconscious before removing a tooth.

"Okay, Kenny, don't worry now," the dentist said, as he placed that hideous rubber gas mask over his face. Kenny was terrified, the mask was probably clean but it felt slimy, as it engulfed his little face. All he could see was the biggest brightest lamp he had ever seen in his life and the dentist's face, as he held that slimy rubber mask over his face. Kenny felt his eye lids start to droop, he tried to fight it, but his eyes closed.

Then his eyes shot wide open again. Kenny found himself standing in a long dimly lit tunnel. Suddenly someone or something grabbed hold of Kenny's jacket and without looking back to see who it was, Kenny fled down the tunnel.

"I just knew I was running for my life," was how Kenny described it to me.

After running a couple of hundred yards, Kenny came upon a wall. Only this was no ordinary wall, it had a strange luminescence about it and Kenny could see that it was made up of layers. He touched the wall and gently scratched the surface; it came away like soft cheese. He really didn't want to, but something was compelling him to scratch away at the wall. Soon a football sized hole had been scraped out of the first layer and just as Kenny broke through to the second layer, a bright light burst into his eyes.

"Kenny, wake up! you are at the dentist. Your mum is waiting for you. Are you ok?"

The dentist's face slowly emerged from that intense light and Kenny coughed on a large clot of blood in his throat. "Here, sit up and spit it into this little sink and drink some water," the dentist soothed. "That's it, that's a good boy."

Kenny fled into his mother's arms with a wad of cotton wool in his mouth.

"Oh, come on, my brave boy," his mother hugged, "Let's get you home and give you some jelly and ice cream."

The jelly and ice cream was delicious to this scared little boy, who found himself back in that dark tunnel any time he tried to sleep. The following Thursday, it was time for Kenny to have his second tooth taken out and he begged his mum not to make him go through with it.

"You will be fine, you are my brave boy."

Once again Kenny had to endure the agony of that big bright light and the dentist's face, as he plunged that slimy rubber mask over his face. Kenny tried so hard to stay awake and he felt as though his eyes had only just fully closed, when they shot wide open again. There was no running down a tunnel this time. He was standing in front of the wall and the football sized hole that he had scraped out of the first layer was there too.

He really did not want to do it, but he felt compelled to scratch away at the second layer. Once again, as Kenny broke through the second layer and into the third, a bright light hit his eyes and the dentist was waking him up. And so it continued into the third and fourth week, with Kenny praying for the last tooth to be removed. So he would not have to scrape away at the wall anymore.

As the dentist extracted Kenny's fifth tooth, Kenny was standing in front of the wall again. Thank God he only had to endure this three more times. But as Kenny started to scratch away at layer number five, he realised something that froze his blood. There were only two more layers left after this one and only two more teeth to come out.

The sixth tooth was taken out the following Thursday and Kenny couldn't sleep for a week leading up to the final extraction. Why do dentists call it that? It sounds so sinister. He continuously badgered his mum not to make him go through with the last extraction, but she would not hear of it. Her 'Brave Boy' had been very strong and he was going to see this through.

Kenny lay back in the dentist's chair for the final time.

"I bet you are glad this is the last time you will see me?" the dentist smiled.

Kenny did not even bother to answer him. His heart pounded in his chest as the dentist placed that disgusting slimy rubber mask over his face. His eyes closed, and then shot wide open. The Wall. One layer to go.

As on every other occasion, Kenny desperately did not want to scratch away at the wall, but could not help himself. As he finally broke through the final layer, Kenny prayed for the bright light to hit his eyes and the dentist to be waking him up. But there was nothing. He pushed a fist sized hole through the last layer of the wall and looked through, but all he could see was black darkness. He scraped away the rest of the football sized hole and looked through again. At first it looked like pitch darkness and then Kenny's eyes grew accustomed to the dark.

"That's when I saw him," Kenny told me.

"Who?"

"Death!"

"Death?"

"Yeah, you know him, Death."

"What do you mean? Death?"

"If I asked you to come up with an image of Death in your mind, what it would it be?" Kenny asked.

"Probably the Grim Reaper in a black hooded robe and a scythe," I replied.

"Exactly," Kenny said, "Except he didn't have a scythe, just him in that black robe with his hood up, and you could just make out his black eyes."

Kenny literally felt his heart stop pumping in his chest.

Kenny turned to run away and then froze on the spot. Death was standing right behind him!

With the speed of lightening, Death seized Kenny round the throat with one hand and started to throttle him. Kenny felt his feet leave the floor and desperately tried to fight back, but he felt like he was back in one of his dreams. The dreams he has of fighting the school bully, but no matter how hard he tries to hit the bully, his arms feel like they are made of lead.

As Kenny felt the life draining from his body, Death hit him hard across the face with the back of his hand. Death's face closed in on Kenny and snarled, as he slapped Kenny across the face again.

The bright light hit Kenny in the eyes and he frantically

kicked out and punched the air, as he screamed for his life.

"Kenny! It's Okay, Kenny, your mum is here. It's okay, calm down."

The dentist's face came into view, along with another man, an older man with half-moon, wire framed spectacles. Kenny wretched and threw up a mixture of blood and bile all over the dentist's white tunic. The dentist gently lifted Kenny's head and encouraged him to 'spit it all out and drink some water.'

As Kenny was getting his breath back, he heard the dentist whisper to the older man, "That was close."

"Yes, too close," the older man replied. "You had better send his mother to see me straight away."

As the old man left the room, Kenny's mum was brought in. Both she and Kenny knew there was something wrong, as Kenny's mum had never been allowed into the dentist's operating room before. Kenny threw his arms around his mum's waist, as she begged the dentist to tell her what was going on.

"Kenny is fine, Mrs Birchall. We just had a little hiccup, that's all and I had to call upon Dr Sidcup from the GP surgery downstairs. I know he is not your GP, but he needs to speak to you straight away."

Kenny and his mum were shown into Dr Sidcup's sumptuous office and each took a seat, in front of his magnificent desk. Neither Kenny nor his mother dared to speak, as Dr Sidcup studied some papers on his desk.

"Mrs Birchall, I see that your GP is Dr Gosling. Dr Gosling is a very good friend of mine. With your permission, I am going to write to Dr Gosling and suggest that he refers Kenny to the hospital for some tests."

"What sort of tests?" Kenny's Mother gasped.

"Oh, I am sure it is nothing to worry about," the doctor tried to assure Kenny's mother. "I would just recommend that you make an appointment at the hospital to get Kenny's heart checked out. It may have just been the affects of the anaesthetic, but Kenny's heart stopped for a short time today."

Just when Kenny thought his nightmare was over, he had to go to hospital. His mum promised him there would be no more gas masks and no more being put to sleep. The tests at the hospital could not find any problems with Kenny and to this day, Kenny does not know whether his experience was nothing more than gas induced dreams, or something a lot more sinister.

Something none of us even dare to contemplate.

AUTHOR'S NOTES

After leaving school aged 16 with no qualifications, well one, in woodwork! Carle O'Hare went away to sea in the Merchant Navy.

Starting out as 'The Galley Boy' his job was to wash the pots and pans and peel potatoes. He did however get to travel the world meeting the most amazing characters. Not least of all 'Old Shaun' and his dead best friend Shamus!

Carle then moved to Dover and worked for cross channel ferry company Townsend Torresen, on board a ship called,

'The Herald of Free Enterprise' as a member of C watch.

'C watch' was also filled with amazing characters, all great friends of Carle. Sadly most of them lost their lives on the night of March the 6th 1987, when an unbelievable series of events led to the Herald capsizing with the loss of 193 passengers and crew.

Carle went home to Liverpool and completed a Psychology degree at John Moores University, Liverpool. Whilst studying, Carle began work as a taxi driver and one particular module of his studies grabbed his attention. The Psychology of the Paranormal. Although having never seen a ghost himself, Carle recalled strange tales he heard from his days at sea. Friends and family also told Carle fascinating paranormal stories and Carle found himself asking his taxi customers,

"Have you ever seen a ghost?" Usually the answer would be, "No...........but!

The idea of writing the collection of stories into a book began to form and then one day Carle heard Billy Butler (BBC Merseyside) inviting listeners to attend a presentation on writing and publishing at the BBC studios as part of their 'Up for Arts' programme. The presenter was best selling thriller writer, Conrad Jones, who has produced 13 gritty crime novels set in Liverpool since 2008. That event led to this book being published!.